DOGGED PURSUIT

ALSO BY DAVID ROSENFELT

DOGGED PURSUIT

David Rosenfelt

MINOTAUR BOOKS

NEW YORK

First published in the United States by Minotaur Books, an imprint of St. Martin's Publishing Group

DOGGED PURSUIT. Copyright © 2025 by Tara Producti⟨
All rights reserved. Printed in the United States of A⟨
For information, address St. Martin's Publishing G⟨
120 Broadway, New York, NY 10271.

www.minotaurbooks.com

The Library of Congress Cataloging-in-Publicatior
is available upon request.

ISBN 978-1-250-32451-1 (hardcover)
ISBN 978-1-250-32452-8 (ebook)

Our books may be purchased in bulk for promotional, educational, or business use. Please contact your local bookseller or the Macmillan Corporate and Premium Sales Department at 1-800-221-7945, extension 5442, or by email at MacmillanSpecialMarkets@macmillan.com.

First Edition: 2025

10 9 8 7 6 5 4 3 2 1

AUTHOR'S NOTE

Regular readers of the Andy Carpenter books may notice some chronology issues in this book as it relates to Andy's life and history. All this is due to the fact that while golden retrievers live far too short lives, Tara will be the exception to that rule. So I do apologize, but when it comes to a choice between totally accurate chronology and Tara's living forever, it's an easy decision.

DOGGED
PURSUIT

It was a twice-a-year event that spanned decades.

Stephen Pearson would throw a party for his employees, a gathering that both showed his appreciation for their hard work and also contributed to company camaraderie.

Since the company, Pearson Trucking, was based in Paterson, New Jersey, the venue of choice for the party was always Morelli's, an outstanding bar/restaurant on Market Street. Morelli's was a fixture in Paterson, going back even further than Pearson Trucking.

The parties never drew more than thirty or thirty-five people, not even half of the eighty-five employees of the company. That's because most of the employees were truck drivers and therefore many were often out on the road when the events took place.

Stephen felt it important to continue the tradition established by his late father, Walter, the company's founder. Stephen did this even through rough times; in fact, just two years ago the business had faced an existential financial crisis. But still they partied on, and now Pearson Trucking was back on much firmer footing.

Stephen had recently laid off three employees, two drivers and one office worker. The reason given was a cutback in overhead costs, though the fired employees disputed that. One in particular, a longtime employee and friend of Stephen Pearson's, got into a heated argument with him. The fired employee went so far as to warn Pearson that he would regret what he had done.

That employee was Ryan Tierney, and for obvious reasons he was not at Morelli's that night.

As was always the case, the more beer that was consumed, the more people relaxed and tended to forget it was a work function. Pearson ultimately gave his typical party speech, telling the assembled group how proud he was of the work they were doing, and predicting great things in the future.

The party started breaking up at around eleven o'clock. Pearson was one of the last to leave, as usual. He wanted to make sure that everyone who had a car there was fit to drive. Often he wound up driving some people home, which he was fine doing.

He was worried for their safety and didn't fully trust them to take a cab. He also realized he could have some legal liability as their host if they got into an alcohol-induced accident.

It was close to midnight when he got ready to leave, along with two other colleagues. One, a woman, was his assistant, and the other was a man who handled IT issues as well as other technical problems that came up in the office.

Pearson had parked his car behind the restaurant, and the three of them headed back there together. Pearson was fine; he never had more than one beer. The other two seemed okay as well, though the IT man probably was technically over the legal blood alcohol level.

The three reached the car. The woman got into the front passenger seat, and the man got in the back behind Pearson, who was of course the driver.

He turned the key and their lives were ended instantly in a fiery explosion.

'm an adult.

I take no pleasure in saying that; it certainly wasn't my first choice. I fought it off as long as I could. But it's an inevitable result of living past one's teenage years, and I've finally had to concede.

Adulthood has claimed another victim . . . Andy Carpenter.

I'm almost thirty years old, so I know that most people would think I crossed the maturity threshold a while back. But I didn't accept it mentally; I kept thinking I'd wake up in the fraternity house, bleary-eyed from a night of poker, tequila, and beer, and some time on the bathroom floor throwing up. That is what now qualifies as the good old days.

The biography, such as it is, doesn't lie. I graduated from NYU Law School, then worked for three years in the prosecutor's office in Passaic County, New Jersey. I will admit that there might have been some nepotism involved; before he retired, my father, Nelson, was the chief prosecutor and the man who ran the office. But he took a hands-off attitude to my hiring, and his top deputy, Richard Wallace, handled it.

I got married almost a year ago to Nicole Gant, who even after the marriage remained Nicole Gant. I can't say I blame her. Her father, Senator Philip Gant, is enormously wealthy and is probably New Jersey's leading citizen. It's not a last name one would give up easily.

The Gant family goes back as far as a family can go, probably to the *Mayflower*. In fact, based on their accumulation of
money and their attitude about it, it's likely they owned the
Mayflower and sold cruise tickets to the other passengers on
board. They would have charged extra for the newly invented
Thanksgiving buffet, and rooms that faced the Rock as they
pulled into Plymouth must have gone for a fortune.

Nicole and I are separated, or at least I think we are. We
never specifically assigned that name to it, but we haven't
been getting along well and we mutually decided that she
should spend some time at a family beach house.

She's on Long Beach Island, although there are few beaches
where that family does not have a house. We still communi-
cate on a fairly regular basis, and she's been making statements
that indicate she's coming home. But nothing so far, and she's
been there for almost three weeks.

The natural order of things feels like it's been turned on
its head. It seems like I have known Nicole forever, and from
the moment we met I think we both knew we'd wind up
together. I'm not sure when familiarity turned to love, but it
definitely did . . . for both of us.

I miss her and I hope this "sort-of-separation" brings us
back to where we were.

We live, or for the moment I should say I live, in Franklin
Lakes, New Jersey. It's about twenty minutes from Paterson,
which is where I grew up, and where my father still lives.
My mother passed away last year. I would rather be living in
Paterson, but moving to comfortable suburbia is a concession
I made for Nicole.

Nicole's father actually built a house for us on his estate,
but I convinced Nicole that living so close to them would be

less than an outstanding idea. So we declined, and the Gants now use it as a fairly spectacular guesthouse.

I do have an office in Paterson, which I took three months ago when I opened my practice as a defense attorney. It's a bit of a dump above a fruit stand on Van Houten Street, but I got a good deal on the place. My landlord is Sofia Hernandez, the owner of the fruit stand, and I negotiated to get her to throw in a monthly bag of peaches in the summer and apples in the winter.

It's definitely not the kind of place to show off to clients. Of course, that hasn't been a problem, since so far I've only had one client.

Her name is Darla Grimes, or at least that is her professional name. She's an exotic dancer and a sex worker, so it was no surprise that she was arrested for prostitution for the fourth time. The first three times she was not represented by me, which is why she pled guilty and took probation and a fine.

This time they were not going to be so lenient and were seeking jail time. So I told her to plead not guilty and I informed the prosecutors that we'd go to trial. I would say they were both annoyed and amused at my stand; actual trials in these situations are few and far between.

They thought I must be nuts, but they didn't know me because the case was in Bergen County and I had worked in the Passaic County office. If they knew me, they would have known for sure that I'm nuts.

In the pretrial motions I informed the court that I would be calling a group of character witnesses, people who had done business with Darla in her "professional" capacity. The judge asked me to provide the names, but I said that it was a delicate matter, and I hadn't made specific decisions yet. But I did say that subpoenas would be necessary; these would not be cooperating witnesses.

I informed the court that I envisioned a two-week trial and mentioned that I had a large list from which I would choose people to call, when in fact I had no list. I reemphasized that it was a delicate matter, and the judge was fine with waiting.

Within twenty-four hours someone in the Bergen County hierarchy decided that heck, poor Darla deserved another chance. This left me with a one-case winning streak and left Darla free to ply her trade until the next arrest.

I have a feeling that arrest won't come for quite a while. But just in case, I'm going to keep the nonexistent list in the nonexistent safe in my new office.

Today is a big day for me . . . I'm going to get a dog. Maybe.

I've wanted a dog for a while; in fact, I've wanted one my entire life. When I was growing up, all my friends had them and doted on them. There has always been something about dogs that I connected to; it didn't matter what size or breed.

But my mother was allergic to them, or so she said, so it wasn't possible while I was living at home. I told her there are dogs that are nonallergenic, but she did not seem moved by the information. Begging never helped, and I was never able to enlist my father to the cause.

After college I was a single guy in an apartment, and I didn't think it would be fair to a dog to be stuck all day by himself. So I fought the urge and put it off until my situation changed.

Unfortunately, when I got married, Nicole really didn't want one, though she didn't outright refuse to go along with it. She's never had a dog, and I think the prospect scares her a bit. But I still haven't gotten one because I've been sort of honoring her hesitancy, even though she had recently indicated a tentative willingness to go along.

So I think she will be okay with what I'm planning for today.

I'm going down to the Passaic County Animal Shelter to

check out the dogs that are there. I haven't definitely made the decision to get one; I just figure I'll know when I know. But just going to the shelter represents, at least in my mind, a significant step.

I want a small dog, no bigger than twenty pounds. That's partially because they tend to be cute, but also because a dog that size would be easier for Nicole to handle. Her fear of dogs is directly proportional to their size, possibly because little dogs have smaller teeth.

I've been to this shelter before to interview the shelter manager, Ralph Brandenberger, for some animal abuse cases we were prosecuting. I insisted on jail time for the guilty scumbags in all those cases and got it in every one of them. I would actually have been okay with the death penalty, but the judges wouldn't go along.

Ralph is waiting for me at the door when I arrive; I had called to tell him I was coming. He seemed happy to hear I might be adopting; every time he can get a dog out of this place is a win.

"I want a little dog," I say.

"How little?"

"Maybe twenty pounds, max. Probably less."

"Okay." He takes me to the kennel area, and the dogs start to bark when they hear us coming. "Back there," he says, pointing toward the end of a long corridor with dog runs on both sides. "That's where the little guys are."

I have to gird myself for this and make sure I look straight ahead. I don't want to see the dogs that we are going to pass. I know I can't take them, and I'll feel terrible about it, so better I don't see them.

Unfortunately, I hear a noise to my left and I involuntarily turn to look. It's a run with two dogs in it. The one that made the noise is a beagle, and it is barking and nudging against the cage, as if hoping to receive some attention, a few scratches and a pat on the head.

But that's not the one I'm looking at. A few feet farther back is a beautiful golden retriever, not moving toward me, just watching me. I look at the card on the outside of the cage and I see that she's a female.

I know this will sound weird, but instantly I feel like I understand this dog. She is telling me that I am not needed; that she will do quite well with or without me. She is stuck in this awful situation and yet conveys a dignity that stuns me.

I have never before seen this dog, but I've known her my entire life. That's how instant and powerful the connection is.

She does not belong here and she is not going to stay here. She belongs with me . . . end of discussion.

Ralph has walked ahead, thinking I am with him, then stops when he realizes that I came to a halt well behind him. He comes back to me and I say, "I want her."

"You may have noticed she's not a little dog."

"I already figured that out. What do you know about her?"

"Her name is Tara. That's pretty much it."

"How did you get her?"

"Someone dropped her off about two weeks ago in the morning, before we were open. He tied her up outside and left a note asking us to please take care of her. The note said she was wonderful, but the person couldn't keep her anymore. He or she didn't say why."

"She's mine, effective immediately."

"You want to go in a room and spend time with her?"

"I don't need to."

"Good enough," he says, then turns to the other dog in the run. "I'm sorry, Sonny, but your friend is leaving."

"They're friends?"

He nods. "Yeah. They seem bonded."

My mouth starts talking before consulting with my brain. "Then I'll take him also."

"Sorry, Andy. No can do."

"Why not?"

"Come on in my office and I'll tell you about it."

"Okay, let's bring my dog. Come on, Tara."

Ralph takes Tara out of the run, leaving Sonny looking upset and lonely, or at least that's my impression. He's staring at me like it's my fault, and he's right about that.

We go into Ralph's office and he tells me that Sonny is under a legal hold, which is a situation I am familiar with. His owner, a man named Ryan Tierney, is in jail and awaiting trial, though Ralph does not know the details of the situation. The name sounds familiar to me, but I can't quite place it.

Per the law, Sonny must stay in the custody of the county until the case is adjudicated. Sometimes these things can take a long time, no matter what the offense. If Tierney gets off, the dog goes back to him. If not, the county takes possession.

"So there's nothing I can do," Ralph says. "It's a shame; he's a great dog and he doesn't deserve this."

"What if this Tierney guy signs a letter turning him over to me? Then you don't have to worry about waiting for the owner's case to be resolved because I'd be the owner."

Ralph thinks for a while. "I don't know. I probably should consult a lawyer."

"Here's a happy coincidence. I'm a lawyer; consult away."

He smiles. "You don't think I'll get in trouble?"

"If you do, I'll defend you right up until the moment they put you in the electric chair. And I'll even reduce my fee, though of course I would expect it to be paid in advance."

He laughs. "You think you can get Tierney to agree?"

"I'll make him an offer he can't refuse." Then, "Tell Sonny Tara and I will be back for him as soon as we can."

head home with Tara in the backseat; she seems comfortable back there.

I think she's pleased with the recent developments; she has a smile on what is nothing less than a perfect face.

My plan is to go home and find out what I can about Ryan Tierney before approaching him in the jail. I'll only have one shot at talking him into letting me have Sonny.

While I'm driving, I look in the rearview mirror and the view is blocked by Tara's head; she is standing up. I probably should have put a seat belt on her, but I'm new at this.

I'm struck by how large she seems; not exactly the small dog I was planning to get. "Tara, you're probably going to meet Nicole soon," I say. "When you do, scrunch down a lot and try to look as small as possible."

Before we go in the house I take her for a walk. Ralph had given me a couple of plastic bags, which quickly become necessary. This is one house-trained dog.

I know it's strange, but I talk to her along the way. I tell her that she will never have to go back to that shelter, that she is now a member of the family. I assure her that nothing bad will ever happen to her again.

She doesn't answer; she just sniffs the ground and takes in her surroundings. But she smiles a lot and wags her tail, so I'm thinking she understands and is okay with it.

I add, "And I'm going to get your friend Sonny out of that dump."

The first step toward doing that is to google whatever information I can find out about Tierney's case. In a perfect world, he'd be in for jaywalking and be released this afternoon. That way Sonny would be fine and I wouldn't have to have two dogs when I wanted one.

It takes me all of three minutes on the computer to learn that while Tierney may well have been jaywalking, the prosecutors must have decided not to charge him with it. They clearly would have felt that charging him with multiple murders is more than sufficient to put him away. Because as soon as I start reading, I remember where I heard the name Ryan Tierney.

Tierney was an employee of a company called Pearson Trucking, based in Paterson. It seems to be a fairly large company, with a fleet of more than fifty trucks, though I have no idea where that would rank them among their competitors.

The founder of the company was Walter Pearson, and when he died nine years ago, his son Stephen took over. There's going to have to be another management change, though, since Stephen is one of the people Ryan Tierney is accused of murdering.

According to the articles, Tierney had been fired from his job two weeks before the murders, which screams "motive." The murder took place in the parking lot behind Morelli's Restaurant in Paterson. Leaving the place after a company party, Pearson and two of his colleagues died in an explosion when he turned on the ignition in his car.

Because of that motive, and because it was Pearson's car that blew up, it seems that the police consider the two other people to have been in the wrong place at the wrong time. They're clearly being chalked up to collateral damage.

The event was obviously big news in Paterson, and the arrest was widely covered as well. I hadn't followed it too closely since I had no idea I'd be trying to rescue the accused's dog. It didn't penetrate deep into my consciousness, but I remember it struck me as possibly mob related because of the car bomb. After all, Michael Corleone's wife in Italy was killed the same way.

There is a mention that Tierney is being represented by the public defender in Paterson, so my next move is to call Billy Cameron, known to everyone as Bulldog. Billy is the head of the Public Defender's office, so I got to know him some when I was a prosecutor.

We tangled a couple of times on cases, both of which I won. It had nothing to do with my legal genius; I had all the facts on my side.

Billy wasn't bitter about the defeats, mainly because I spent a lot of our downtime asking him about his college football exploits. Billy was a wide receiver for the University of Georgia, and he loves to talk about the time he caught four touchdown passes in a winning effort against Auburn.

It's understandable; if I had caught four touchdown passes in an SEC game, I would have the box score tattooed on my forehead.

"So I hear you moved over to the side of truth and justice," he says when I get him on the phone. He considers the defense side to be the righteous one.

"Somebody had to; you keep screwing up your cases."

He laughs. "How does your father feel about the move?" He knows that as a lifelong, now-retired prosecutor, my father must be horrified at having his only son turn traitor.

"He's pretending to be supportive; but I think he's claiming to his friends that I was adopted."

Another laugh, then, "So what can I do for you?"

"I want to talk to Ryan Tierney."

"You want the case?" Billy asks, a little too eagerly. It could mean he thinks it's a sure loser, or more likely he just wants to reduce the crushing workload that the Public Defender's office always labors under. A murder case would be a time killer, especially one of this magnitude.

"No, thank you, but I deeply appreciate the offer and your obvious confidence in me. It's a real morale booster."

"So why do you want to talk to him?"

"I want to adopt his dog."

"Well, this is a first. What the hell are you talking about?"

So I tell Billy what I'm talking about and he says, "I didn't know you were a dog person."

"I'm not. I just can't let this dog rot in a cage because his owner killed a bunch of people."

"You're on the defense side now, Andy. He is alleged to have killed a bunch of people. And he's innocent until proven guilty; you might want to familiarize yourself with that concept."

"So can you get me in to see your innocent client?"

"Sure. He'll be glad to have the company."

Ryan Tierney has a different reaction to me from that of other accused criminals I have interviewed here.

That is obviously because in the past I represented the enemy, the person who was trying to put them away for a long time. Invariably it was in the presence of their attorney, possibly to discuss a plea bargain or a chance that the accused would turn on an accomplice and testify for the government.

But Billy Cameron, or someone in his office, obviously told Tierney that I represented no such threat, so he doesn't show the wariness I've come to expect. He's not smiling and warm; his situation doesn't call for it. But I'm not feeling any hostility.

That's the first thing I notice when Tierney is brought into the meeting room. The second thing is his size. I guess I expected a truck driver accused of murder to be a big guy, rough and intimidating.

Tierney is anything but that. He looks like my high school English teacher, the one who never succeeded in getting me to like or understand poetry. I think that's because poetry was always something to be deciphered, and I prefer straight talk.

If people generally write the way they speak, I'd hate to get stuck sitting next to a poet at a baseball game.

Hey, Walt Whitman . . . you got something to say, just say it.

"Is Sonny okay?" Tierney asks, before he even sits down.

"Yes. Why do you ask?"

"Mr. Cameron said you wanted to talk to me about Sonny. I was worried."

"He's fine. He's at the Passaic County Animal Shelter."

Tierney shakes his head. "Damn. That's what I was afraid of. I got him out of that place two years ago, and I promised him he'd never have to go back."

I'm instantly feeling sorry for Tierney; he may or may not be a murderer, but he's definitely a dog lover. And he clearly agrees with me that the beagle should not have to pay for the sins of the human. So it is written, so it shall be.

"You have any family that might take him?"

He shakes his head. "No, it's just me."

"I understand. I just rescued a dog from there that was in the same run as Sonny. I was willing to take Sonny as well because the two dogs really like each other. But they wouldn't let me."

"Why?"

"Because he's your dog and by law they have to wait until your case is resolved. Then if you can take him, fine. If not, he's theirs and they make the decisions."

"That's not fair to him."

"I agree, which is why I'm here. You can sign an agreement giving up your rights to him, in which case they will let me have him. Otherwise he's stuck there."

"I can't do that. I am innocent, and when I get out of here . . ."

"I don't want two dogs. I'm just providing a short-term solution to his situation. He's yours again when you get out."

He looks at me warily. "What if you change your mind?"

"I won't, but that's a chance you're taking. The alternative is him spending a long time in that dump, even if you win your case."

"Okay, I'm in. I just worry about him."

"I get it, but you're doing the right thing."

He nods. "I'm scared I won't get out of here . . . I mean never. I don't think I can handle that. I did not kill those people."

"Then Billy's team will prove it."

He frowns. "I don't think so. They seem to have so much going on; I've only talked to them a few times." Then, "Mr. Cameron said you're a lawyer, and that you might take my case."

"Oh, he did?"

"He said you're the best."

Note to self . . . kill Billy Cameron. "I'm not the best . . . not even close."

"Then why would he say that?"

"The truth? Because they're overworked; too many clients, too few lawyers."

He nods. "That's why I want you as my lawyer. Do you have too many clients?"

I decide not to tell him that if I took on his case, that would make a total of one. "Not at the moment."

"Then what do you say?"

I need to think about this. If I'm going to be a defense attorney, then I am going to have to have clients to defend. Some will be guilty, some innocent, but all are entitled to a good defense. That's the way the system works, and I am not rich enough to buck it.

But I'm not ready to commit to a case like this. And I have

to think long and hard about how I'd feel defending someone who might have blown up three people. The good defense the system mandates doesn't have to be provided by me.

"I'll talk to Billy," I say.

"Thank you. And please give Sonny a hug for me."

I've got to admit I'm looking forward to seeing Tara when I get home.

I am slightly worried, though. I did not confine her in any way, and she is a dog, so there is always the chance that she has used the house as a chew toy.

Hopefully she didn't get into Nicole's closet. Nicole has shoes and bags so valuable that she could trade a few in for something with bucket seats. But the truth is that an army of golden retrievers would take a month to eat all of Nicole's shoes. She could clothe the feet of the entire Russian army, though I suspect they'd start limping around a lot.

It may be an ominous sign that when I open the door, Tara is not there to greet me. I was hoping for a tail-wagging golden, eager to shower me with affection, but that's not what I get. Nothing is what I get.

I'm worried as I search for her, but that search doesn't take too long. She's on the couch in the den, lying in Nicole's lap as Nicole strokes her head. Tara barely looks at me when I walk into the room; actually neither of them do.

"I see you two have met." Then I turn to Tara. "Traitor."

Nicole smiles. "We have. She's wonderful. If I had to be replaced, you've made an excellent choice."

"You weren't replaced. But I'm very glad you like her. And I'm very glad you're home."

She nods. "Yes, this is home." Then, "Where did you get her?"

I tell her the story, and I cringe a little when I add the part about Sonny and the possibility that we could be a two-dog household for a while.

"So another one is coming?" she asks, with little enthusiasm.

"Yes, it looks like that. But only for a while, as long as I can get my client acquitted. He owns her."

"You have a client already?"

I nod. "I think so; not officially but I'm leaning that way. And I think you'd like him."

"The client?"

"No, the dog."

"What is the client accused of?"

"Multiple murders."

"Sounds delightful. Andy, have you thought more about my father's offer?"

"I have." Nicole's father wants me to be a corporate lawyer in the family company. "I even spoke to him about it."

"And?"

"And he was somewhat annoyed when I declined, even though I did it with a great deal of charm."

"Why don't you want to do it?"

I think for a moment. "How should I put this? Imagine having a root canal every day for the rest of your life, except on Fridays, when they do the extractions."

She laughs. "You didn't put it that way to my father, did you?"

"No. I'm stubborn, not courageous. I let him down gently, though I must admit he isn't used to being let down at all." Then, "Are you going to stay awhile?"

She nods. "Hopefully forever. Andy, I know we've had a rocky start, but I want to make this work."

"Good. So do I." I walk over and pet Tara's head, which is still resting in Nicole's lap. "Let's do it for the children."

Y ou set me up," I say to Billy when I get him on the phone.

He laughs; I don't think I have him fully intimidated. "I sure did. Did it work?"

"Very likely. But I do want to see the discovery."

"I'll have it sent over right away; you have an office?"

"Actually I do." I give him the Van Houten Street address and tell him it's on the second floor above the fruit stand. "You make a left just past the bananas and go up the stairs."

"Very impressive."

"I can get summer fruit long before you can even dream of it." Then, "Also send me a transcript of the arraignment."

"I will, but it was uneventful. He pled not guilty and has said he's not interested in a deal. So you may have a trial on your hands."

"Does he by any chance have any money to pay his lawyer?"

"Obviously not; we're public defenders, remember? We can't even get summer fruit. But I can pay you out of our budget; we're set up to hire outside counsel. You'll make a lot more than the lawyers who work here, but please don't mention that to them. And there's also a decent budget for investigators and expert witnesses."

"Okay. Once I've gone through the discovery, you can file with the court that you're withdrawing as counsel and I'm taking over. You can tell them that my first act as lead counsel was to fire you."

"Great. You won't regret this . . . or maybe you will. But I sure won't."

I get up and ask Tara if she wants to go for a ride. She immediately jumps up and starts wagging her tail. I've got a feeling this is one smart dog. "Good," I say. "Let's go get your friend."

We go back to the shelter and Ralph sees us walk in. "You're not bringing her back, are you?" he asks, meaning Tara.

"Are you nuts? No chance."

"Great," he says, obviously relieved. "Did you speak to Tierney?"

"I did; here's the release letter."

He smiles. "Now this is what I call a good day. Let's go get Sonny."

"You go. I don't want Tara to have to go back there; I don't want her to think I'm giving her back."

"Okay. You want any other dogs while you're here? You're on a roll."

"No, thanks. Two should do it."

Ralph brings Sonny out, and within a few seconds Tara and Sonny are wagging their tails and sniffing each other's asses. It's probably not the greatest idea to bring them home and dump them off with Nicole, so I take them down to the office to wait for the discovery to arrive.

When I get to the office, Sam Willis is waiting for me. Sam is my accountant and friend, and he has an office down the hall from mine. He's the one who told me about the vacancy. Maybe he even got a watermelon as a finder's fee.

Sam is an unusual character; emphasis on both *unusual* and *character*. I've known him for about ten years; we had a friend in common who recommended him as an accountant when I got out of college.

In his spare time he teaches computer science at William Paterson University and also a senior class in it at the local Y. He's a genius on computers and considers the internet his home. When I once asked if he meant "second home," he said no, that his real-life home occupies that second-place spot.

When he was twelve years old his father gave him a computer for his birthday, and he says he's never looked back, that it changed his life and he became brilliant at computer science. My father gave me a baseball glove, but it unfortunately did not have a similar result.

Sam also not so secretly yearns to be a detective, and when I told him I was moving to the defense side, he immediately offered his services as my investigator. He told me that he has a license to carry so he could handle himself "on the street."

I had responded, "Let me know which street you're talking about, Sam, so I can take an alternate route."

When I arrive, Sam looks at Tara and Sonny and says, "You seem to have two dogs."

"What tipped you off?"

He doesn't think that's worthy of a response. "Some boxes arrived for you. Your office was locked, so I have them."

Billy has obviously gotten the discovery here at record speed, probably so I wouldn't have time to change my mind.

Sam helps me bring the three boxes into my office and frowns when he sees all the pages. "This stuff should all be digitized."

Sam has made occasional efforts to teach me about the cyber-world. So far I am barely able to turn on my phone and occasionally send emails, so it's fair to say that his success as a tutor has been limited. Teaching me anything about technology is an exercise in futility.

He has also set up a website for me in my new role as defense attorney, and while it looks great, I don't think anybody has seen it. If a website in the cyber-woods gets no traffic, does it make a sound?

The discovery, as I read through it, is quite bad for Ryan Tierney. This is not exactly newsworthy. Based on what is in here, they have charged him with multiple counts of murder. Therefore, one wouldn't expect a bunch of exculpatory evidence.

It's as if you handed in a final exam in school, and when you get it back, there's a big *F* in red on the front. When you skim through it, you're not going to see a lot of positive comments. The failing grade was the decision, and the details fall into line.

In this case, the arrest and indictment was the decision, and the evidence is not going to do anything but support it.

That evidence certainly justified the arrest. The motive, not that they have to prove motive, is that Tierney was fired by Pearson two weeks before the killing. The documents don't come out and say it, but the police and prosecution obviously believe that the other two victims were collateral damage . . . in the wrong place at the wrong time.

Pearson was the target.

There is witness testimony that Tierney was upset, and the two men had a screaming argument when he was fired. Just as damning is that Tierney's car was ticketed two blocks away from the restaurant/bar where the bombing took place.

Apparently that night there was a party thrown by Pearson for his employees at that location; Tierney was obviously not invited because he had been fired. The ticketing happened while the party was in progress and was the result of the car's being parked directly adjacent to a fire hydrant. One of the neighbors called the cops, and they sent someone out to ticket the car.

The cop who wrote the ticket took a photo of the offending car; whoever parked it was practically begging to be ticketed. Also included in the discovery are photos of Tierney's car taken in his driveway the next morning, to demonstrate that it's the same car, license plate and all.

If it's true that the driver was my client, and he illegally parked the car while planting a bomb nearby, then I am unlikely to find a Rhodes Scholarship in his background.

But the real evidence against him is contained in the forensics. The materials that were used in the bomb were basically those used in standard fireworks, just of an amount and intensity to magnify the explosive power.

Those same materials were found during the execution of a search warrant on Tierney's home. He is said, according to the documents, to be an expert on fireworks creation and in fact had a side business where he sold them and put on shows to make extra money.

On its face it looks quite grim for Tierney, but at the same time I realize that I need to work on changing my perspective. I used to work on preparing documents like this from the other side, but that's not where I am now.

I'm a defense attorney, so it's my job to look at this skeptically and to poke holes in it. And there will definitely be holes; there always are. That will be true whether or not Tierney is guilty; no case is without its flaws and weaknesses. So my job is to find the holes and drive a truck through them.

Lucky my client is a truck driver.

That I am on the defense side, rather than the prosecution, is obviously the biggest change for me.

But the second biggest involves the difference in resources. When working for the county, there was always an ample supply of attorneys, office help, police detectives, forensics people, expert witnesses, and so forth to back up the lead attorney.

In addition, while Passaic County will never be confused with Beverly Hills, the available financial resources dwarf those of any defense counsel, especially me.

All this works against the accused; the so-called even playing field is built on a permanent tilt.

But for now our side is just me. I've been considering hiring an assistant, someone to do office stuff, typing, and so on. A friend has recommended a woman named Edna; he says she's a dynamo who loves to work. I'll interview her at some point when I have time.

I'm also going to need an investigator; there is no way I can handle a case of this magnitude on my own. I need to get to that as soon as possible.

When I leave the office, I head for the house I grew up in on Forty-second Street in Paterson. My father lives there alone now; he occasionally says he'll sell it and downsize, but I know he won't. I would certainly hate to see it in someone else's hands; it contains many great memories for me.

Nelson Carpenter is something of a legend in the Paterson legal community; when he retired last year, I spent about a month going to dinners that honored him. He certainly deserved the plaudits; my concern was whether he would go nuts in retirement.

In the year since I wouldn't say he's gone nuts, but he's clearly more than a little bored. I try to come over as often as I can, and even though he says it's not necessary, I know he welcomes the company. We also occasionally go to baseball games together. He's a Yankee fan, something we do not have in common.

This is the first time I've brought dogs with me, but when I tell him the story, he takes it in stride. "I always wished your mother wasn't allergic to them," he says, and then smiles. "Even though she never sneezed when we passed them on the street."

"I've always wondered if that was a scam."

He nods. "Entirely possible. But she took the secret to her grave."

We head into the den, and within seconds Tara has her head in my father's lap so that he pretty much has no choice but to pet her. I swear she gives me a little smile that says that she is in total control.

That's fine with me.

"How's Nicole?" he asks. I knew with 100 percent certainty that would be his first question. He has always liked Nicole, and her father, Senator Philip Gant, is one of his lifelong friends.

I would almost say that Nicole's and my marriage could qualify as arranged. Our respective parents brought us together whenever they had the opportunity, or whenever it was possible to create an opportunity.

At first I think she and I slightly resisted, with an emphasis on *slightly.* Soon we were getting along great; I think that we were from two different worlds increased the appeal. It was cool for each of us to see how the other side lived.

Once, we were supposed to go out but she had to cancel because her mother had the flu, and her father wanted Nicole to accompany him to a state dinner at the White House. I was fine with it, and while she was toasting the prime minister of Great Britain, I sucked down a couple of Big Macs.

But we always got along great; she laughed at my jokes and touched my arm when she talked. What more could anyone want?

"She's fine, Dad, and she even seems to like Tara," I say.

"So she's home?"

I smile. "Yes, she's home. You can breathe easy for the moment. The crisis has passed."

"I just want what's best for you. And speaking of that, you're representing the guy who's accused of killing those people?"My father may have retired, but clearly he was keeping up his connections.

"You don't think that's best for me? And here I thought you'd want to jump aboard as cocounsel."

He ignores that. "Doesn't matter as long as you're going to plead it out."

"That seems unlikely at this point."

"Oh," he says, then lets the silence speak for itself. My father has a way of conveying a lot while saying little. It's one of the reasons he was so good with juries.

"He claims he is innocent." I'm not breaking a client confidence by revealing that; Tierney said the same thing to the police and the judge at the arraignment.

"Really? I've never heard that before. A suspect claiming

innocence; that's breaking new ground. You're in uncharted territory."

"Sometimes it's even true."

"Is this one of those times?"

"Don't know yet; I've just started. But he'll get the best defense I can give him whether it is or not."

I know my father believes in the "innocent until proven guilty" tenet to his core, but I also know that most times the defendant is proven guilty. I also know that he wishes I had never gone over to what he considers the dark side.

"I'm sure you'll do your best," he says. "But to lose a case of this size when you're just starting out . . ."

"I'm aware," I say, allowing him not to have to finish the sentence.

"You know, Andy, you never really told me why you made the switch to the other side."

"Yes, I did. We talked about it."

He shakes his head. "No, you just said you wanted to see if you could make it on your own. But that's a load of crap. . . . It's nonsense you tell your father to try and placate him. You can make it on your own anywhere, no matter how big the organization, or how many people are around you. I made it on my own; nobody handed me anything."

He's right; I've always avoided the subject because I felt that if I told him why I left the prosecutor's office, he might see it as criticizing his decision to spend his life there. But I owe him a real answer.

"Okay, I've spent a few years watching these defendants go down without ever really having a decent chance. I'm not talking about wealthy ones who have the best lawyers; I mean the small-timers who the system runs over. They are the ones who are really on their own.

"I want to give them a shot; I don't need to be another cog in a system that overwhelms them. I'm replaceable in that system, but I'm far less replaceable where I am now. And I don't mean the system is wrong; usually their targets really are guilty. What I am saying is that the system is so strong that guilt or innocence is no longer the determining factor . . . at least not always."

He doesn't respond; he's always had a way of talking by not saying anything. I would love to know what he's thinking, but if he wants to tell me, he will.

While I was talking, he had stopped petting Tara, so she lifts her head and looks at him as if to say, *You can't pet and listen at the same time?* So he resumes the petting and says, "Nice dog you've got here."

I point to Sonny. "So is he. He's just not quite as demanding."

Before I leave my father's, I take Tara and Sonny for a long walk through Eastside Park, which is just about six blocks from the house. I want to give them ample opportunity to do their business before bringing them home.

I'm going to have to leave them with Nicole for a while and I don't want her to discover any accidents on our carpet. I forgot to ask Tierney if Sonny was house-trained, though his performance on our walk through the park makes me believe that he is.

Tara is clearly house-trained; if I didn't walk her, I think she'd use the toilet, flush it, and then wash her paws in the sink afterward.

Nicole is not home when I get there, so I just bring Tara and Sonny into the house, give them water and a couple of biscuits, and then leave. Before I do, I firmly instruct Tara not to do any damage, and to make sure Sonny doesn't either.

Tara turns away from me; I think she's insulted by what I said. This is one smart, sensitive animal. I wanted a dog, and I wound up with an equal.

And I may be giving myself too much credit by saying that.

M orelli's has been closed since the explosion that killed Stephen Pearson and the two others.

That's probably because it's difficult to run a successful restaurant when the entire back wall of your building has been blown away. Among other problems, it would be a bitch to air-condition.

I get there just after 4:00 P.M. and the street feels normal, with everyone just going about their daily business. Morelli's has a simple sign on the front door that says CLOSED FOR RENOVATION . . . THANKS FOR BEARING WITH US.

When I walk around the back, it looks like the Ho Chi Minh trail on a bad day. There is a large hole in the center of the parking lot, poles are down everywhere, and the building itself has sustained substantial damage. It is a good forty feet from the crater, so this was one powerful explosion.

I can't imagine how many pieces they found the victims in, though if this goes to trial, the prosecution will inundate the jury with gruesome photos. It's lucky that it happened at the end of the night when no other people were in the back of the restaurant, or there would have been many more victims.

There is no longer a police presence here and forensics has obviously finished up long ago. I felt I should come here and get a feel for the scene, but I'm not going to learn much, if anything. All there is to commemorate the event is a crater large enough to have killed off the dinosaurs, and a badly damaged restaurant.

I'm about to leave when I see a man coming toward me from inside the building. He literally steps over the rubble as he walks through the wide opening that the explosion caused.

"Can I help you?" he asks.

"I don't think so. I'm investigating what happened here, but it seems fairly obvious."

"Who do you represent?"

"Ryan Tierney."

"Then I don't want to help you."

"Suit yourself, but I'm sorry about what happened. You going to rebuild?"

He nods. "Starting tomorrow. What's your name?"

"Andy Carpenter. And yours?"

"Joseph Morelli."

"So you're the owner?"

"Yeah. Lucky me."

I saw his name in the discovery. "You were here when it happened."

He nods. "The only one. I was going to walk out with Stephen and the others, but I wanted to make sure all the lights were out up front. Otherwise your boy would be facing four murder charges."

"Did Stephen seem worried about anything when he was leaving, or at any time during the night?"

"No. It was a great party. And he was a good guy." Morelli looks out to the crater behind me. "And he did not deserve this. None of them did."

"We can agree on that. Did anything negative happen that night that you noticed? Any arguments between Pearson and one of the guests?"

"You're fishing."

"That's my job description."

He frowns. "Nothing happened. There was a terrific party, everybody had a great time, and then the host's car blew up with three people in it." Then, "And I have half a restaurant."

We talk for a few more minutes, but there's nothing for me to get from him. I'm sure he'll be a witness at trial just to help set the scene, but he won't cause us any real damage. He has no information implicating Tierney.

I leave and walk two blocks down the street and one block over. I'm looking for the place where the car identified as Tierney's was ticketed.

I find the fire hydrant, which is close to the side of a home-owner's driveway. It's as if the driver of the car wanted to make absolutely sure that he'd get a ticket.

If Tierney did this, he is world-class stupid.

I make a mental note to come back here around 10:00 P.M. on a couple of nights to see if there are usually normal parking spots available. I suspect that there are.

That won't prove anything; the prosecution would argue that Tierney was nervous and in a hurry and simply didn't pay attention to where he was parking.

They might even be right.

Nicole actually seems to like the dogs.

She's even located the biscuits and is giving a couple each to Tara and Sonny. They briefly look over at me when I walk in, but keep paying attention to her.

I thought dogs were supposed to be loyal? Where the hell is Lassie when you need her?

"Hey, guys, I'm home! It's me, the one who got you out of that shelter. The one who bought the damn biscuits you're eating."

No response; they couldn't care less. Once Nicole is finished doling out the biscuits, Tara and Sonny walk over to the couch and make themselves at home on it. I think they view this place as an upgrade from the shelter, but I'm not feeling the gratitude.

I know how Sonny wound up there, but I have no idea how Tara did. I cannot imagine anyone stupid enough to give up this dog. What makes it even stranger is that there are no signs that she was mistreated in any way; her coat is nice and she certainly seems comfortable inside a house.

Nicole is an excellent cook and she's made my favorite, pasta amatriciana. It's a major step up from the chicken fingers I've had pretty much every night since she left. Oh, I also threw in a couple of frozen pizzas and some fried rice in a bag. I'm a man of varied tastes.

After dinner, Nicole and I go into the den and share a bottle of wine. This is something that we've always done; it's nice and it's comfortable. Of course, in the past we've never had hairy creatures in our laps, but if anything, that somehow adds to the comfort level.

"Daddy invited us to brunch at the club tomorrow." She always refers to Philip as *Daddy,* rather than *my father.* It's always seemed a bit weird and little girlish to me. I certainly would not refer to Nelson Carpenter as *Daddy.*

"I can't. I have to be at the jail in the morning."

"Why?"

"That's where my client is."

"So you have to work on Saturday?"

"People in jail don't get days off. It's a twenty-four seven job." What I don't tell her is that for a defense attorney in the middle of a murder case, it's also a 24-7 job, or at least close to it. We're going to be turning Daddy down for a lot of brunches, or at least I am.

But for now I'm just going to sit back and enjoy my newly enlarged family. I'm pleased at how accepting Nicole has been to the newcomers, though it's hard to imagine anyone who wouldn't like Tara.

"So, are you going to win your case?" she asks.

"It's going to be an uphill struggle. They always are."

"What kind of a mass murder was it? A shooting? Were there children? . . . No, don't tell me. I want to be able to root for you to win without thinking about who you might be letting out into the streets."

"Fair enough. But no children."

"If you thought he was guilty . . . and don't tell me if you do . . . could you still represent him?"

"Yes. It's my job. It's the way the system works."

"But you're not required to be a part of that system, at least not on this side of it. And not on this case."

"Right . . . it's voluntary. But there are a lot of people on the other side, the prosecution side. It's crowded there; over here it's roomy."

"If you didn't do it, if you weren't his lawyer, the system would find someone else to be on that side."

"I'm better than most of the 'someone elses' the system would find." I believe it, but I'm surprised it came out of my mouth.

"I bet the people on the other side don't have to work on Saturday."

"Most of them don't. You'll probably see them tomorrow at Daddy's brunch at the club."

She frowns, either in dismay or disgust or in grudging appreciation of my humor. I don't think I'll ask which one it was.

thought you forgot about me," Tierney says when he sits down at the table in the meeting room.

His hands are cuffed and chains are on his legs, as is the protocol. He keeps his hands in his lap.

It's only been two days since I saw Tierney, but he's impatient, and I'm sure that to him it has felt a lot longer. "Ryan, here's the thing you need to know. I am working on your case full-time, whether I come here or not."

"Okay, I'm sorry . . . I know. I'm just stressed-out. Every morning when I wake up, it registers with me again that I'm here, and what I am facing."

"I understand. Just hang in there. I need to ask you some questions."

He nods. "Okay."

"You had explosive materials in your basement." It's not a question, but will serve the purpose.

"Yes. To make fireworks. I sold them; I have a license to do so. Just last month I ran the company's July Fourth fireworks display; I do it every year."

"It's the same material that was used in the car explosion."

He looks surprised, which either means he's surprised or he's pretending to be. I don't have the slightest idea which.

"Really?" he asks. "It must have been highly concentrated. But . . ."

"But what?"

"It doesn't make sense. There are so many other materials they could have used without all the work that would have been involved if they used fireworks."

"You know a lot about explosives?"

He nods. "I learned it in the service. I was in ordnance."

That's not good news, except for the prosecution. "Tell me about your relationship with Stephen Pearson."

"We went back a long way, since high school. We were good friends for all those years. Me, and Stephen, and Willie Tirico."

"Who's Willie?"

"We were always together in high school, the three of us. But me and Willie, our families didn't have any money. Stephen was rich, or at least it seemed that way. His father owned the trucking company. Then, when his father died, Stephen took over and hired Willie."

"So Willie started there before you?"

"Yes, I went to work there when I got out of the service."

"Also as a driver?"

"At first just a driver, but then I also pitched in as a dispatcher. After a while dispatcher became more full-time."

"What did that involve?"

"Making sure our trucks were in the right places at the right times. Maximizing efficiency . . . managing the other drivers. It's like moving chess pieces on a board."

"Let's talk about your relationship with the victims. You worked with Denise Clemons?"

"Yes. She started in accounting and then became Stephen's assistant. In that company people did multiple jobs; we were understaffed. Everybody pitched in wherever they were needed."

"You and she got along?"

"Yeah. I mean, I wouldn't call us friends; I didn't know her outside of work at all. But we never had a problem."

"You know anything about her?"

He thinks. "I know she was married to a cop. She once told me he was upset that she had to work so much overtime. He was one of those Neanderthal types; he wanted dinner on the table and stuff like that. I met him at some company functions like that July Fourth thing."

"What about the other victim? Donald Muncy."

He smiles sadly. "Don was a really good guy; I mean, everybody liked him. The kind of guy that brightened up a room, you know?"

"What did he do there?"

"Everything. He was like the office handyman, and he was a whiz on computers and machines. That place would have fallen apart without him."

"And you got along?"

"Absolutely. If you couldn't get along with Don, you had a problem."

"Married?"

He nods. "Yes, with a small child." Then, "I just can't believe all those people are gone. And Stephen . . ."

"Were you surprised when he fired you?"

"I was shocked. I mean, I still don't understand it. I thought the company was doing fine. And Stephen never gave me the slightest hint it was coming."

"What exactly did the business do?"

"Well, we used to truck goods, it didn't matter what kind. Appliances, rolls of fabric, furniture, whatever. We had the trucks and we were in demand. Then it slowed down as more competition entered the market. Stephen felt that we could add another dimension; we could move the possessions of people as they relocated. That way there would be much less time when trucks were idle.

"It worked pretty well; we weren't a leader in the field, but people were discovering us. We were priced well, especially for long-distance moves. But the big change was the refrigeration."

"What does that mean?"

"We started transporting food and groceries. There was a big need for that, especially imports. So we refrigerated part of the fleet to handle it."

"And that was successful?"

He nods. "It was, at least financially."

"But part of it wasn't successful?"

He nods. "I was concerned that we hadn't instituted enough safety procedures. For example, if temperature controls were not right, food could get spoiled. A lot of what we shipped was meat. If it went bad, and people ate it, it could cause huge legal hassles. But I was the only one that seemed concerned."

"So you didn't believe Pearson's reason for firing you?"

"No . . . I still don't."

"And you got angry?"

"Damn right."

"Did you threaten him?"

"Probably. I yelled a lot; he was supposed to be my friend. But it was just talk in the heat of the moment. He wouldn't discuss it with me; it was like he had made up his mind and he refused to hear me. But I swear what I said meant nothing; it was just me letting off steam."

That's not how a jury will see it, but I don't think I'll mention that to him. Instead I will ask the key questions and see how he reacts.

"Where were you while the party was going on?"

"At home."

I already knew what the answer would be; he had said the same thing to the police.

"Nobody saw you? Nobody visited you?"

"No."

"Where was your car?"

"In my driveway."

"It was ticketed for illegal parking two blocks from the restaurant, during the party."

He reacts swiftly. "What? That's not possible."

I know from the transcript of the interview Ryan did with the police that they didn't tell him about the parking ticket; they only asked him where his car was that night. He said it was in his driveway.

"Could someone else have taken it out of your driveway?"

"No, I would have heard. And it's still there, at least as far as I know, so they would have had to bring it back. I would have heard them."

"You're sure?"

"Positive. You need to believe me. How the hell could that have happened?"

"Just another thing we need to find out. Do you have friends at the company that will talk to me?"

"I'm sure I do. They won't believe I could have done this."

I ask him to write out a list with their contact information, which he does.

"How is Sonny doing?" he asks.

I smile. "Living the good life."

There's a sports bar in downtown Paterson that opened a few months ago called Charlie's.

I've heard good things about it, but haven't gotten there yet. That changes tonight.

I've been meaning to check it out, because when football season rolls around, I need a place where I can watch multiple games at once. I'm a big Giants fan, and the two sports highlights of my life were watching Eli Manning beat the Patriots in two Super Bowls.

But it's been a few years since the Giants have had a winning record, and Eli is slowing down. When they fall way behind, I want to have other TVs on which I can watch more competitive games. When the Giants trail by three touchdowns, my loyalty wanes.

I'm meeting Lieutenant Pete Stanton, the number two officer in the Homicide Division of Paterson PD. I got to know Pete when we worked on cases together, though it wasn't always a warm and cuddly relationship. There is nothing warm and cuddly about Pete.

Pete doesn't like lawyers, not even the prosecutors that are on his side. He considers defense attorneys to be pond scum. I imagine that Pete's version of a perfect justice system would consist of permanent incarceration that would begin at the moment Pete decides a suspect is guilty.

I had called Pete and asked if we could meet. I said I wanted to pick his brain, and he suggested I get a brain of my own. But since my father is the only lawyer in the entire world that Pete respects, he agreed to meet me at Charlie's.

Pete is already sitting at a table for two when I arrive, so I walk over, ask, "How's it going?," and then sit down.

He looks at me intently. "Let's be clear about something. You are buying, and I am hungry. And I'm almost as thirsty as I am hungry."

"I've never felt closer to you than I do now."

"Your father disown you yet?"

"You mean because I'm on the defense side?"

"Is there another reason?"

"He's good with it," I say. "He's actually quite proud of me."

"Bullshit."

I nod. "Total."

The waiter comes over and we order. I get a lite beer, hamburger no cheese, and french fries burned beyond recognition.

"You serious?" the waiter asks. "Like, charred?"

"I want them so burned that they would have to run a DNA test to confirm their french fry heritage. So burned that the cook writes a note absolving himself of responsibility."

Pete orders a beer and a steak; he seems unconcerned by price. "So what did you want to talk about?"

"I need to hire an investigator. I know a lot of good people, but they're all connected to the prosecution side."

He is quiet for a moment. "Let me think about it."

He turns to look at the Mets game starting on a few of the TVs. There must be twenty-five TVs within our sight line; this is a place I could see coming to in the future.

Charlie's just has a great feel to it. The best thing I can say about it is that no one here will ever take a picture of their food and post it on Facebook.

I don't know why people do that, and I don't respond to their posts because I have no idea what to say. *Hey, that's a great broccoli spear you've got there!* Or *Wow, that crème brûlée looks so good I'm getting fat just staring at it!*

Charlie's food reminds me of a Richard Farnsworth line from *The Natural.* He's in a restaurant with Redford and says that the food isn't fancy, but "it eats pretty good, don't it?"

It turns out that Pete and I are both Mets fans and Yankee haters, so we're content to watch the game and talk baseball. He had promised to think about potential investigators for me, but if he's actually doing it, he's hiding it well.

Suddenly he says, "Laurie Collins."

"The lieutenant? The really good-looking one?"

"You're married."

"But not blind. What about her?"

"She left the force and is looking to go private. She's a terrific detective."

"Why did she leave?"

"Because the captain she worked under, Dorsey, is an asshole. She decided she didn't want to deal with him anymore. I don't blame her."

I've seen Laurie Collins occasionally, but never worked with her. Maybe we've met once or twice; I'm not sure. She testified for our side in a case I was working on, but I was not the lead attorney and I didn't conduct the direct examination.

"That's a great idea. Thanks."

He nods. "Might be time for you to get the check."

I signal the waiter. "We should do this again sometime."

He nods. "Anytime. Just bring your wallet."

Eric Tanner was more than willing to talk to me. I think I could have suggested we meet at four o'clock in the morning in the fast lane on eastbound Route 80 and he would have been fine with it.

He was the first name on the list of former coworkers that Ryan Tierney gave me, people that he thought would be willing to share what they knew. At this point he's one for one.

We meet at the Forum Diner on Route 4, a place with a menu so large that I think it includes every food item any human has ever eaten, anywhere, at any point in history. That makes it a typical Jersey diner. When I come here, it always takes me a half hour to scan the menu, and then I order a hamburger and a side of fries.

I won't do that today because it's ten o'clock in the morning. The hamburger switch-on time for both me and McDonald's is ten thirty.

As soon as I walk in the door, a man standing off to the side asks, "Mr. Carpenter?" He either knew what I look like, or he has approached every other male customer to enter in the same way. It's probably the latter, because when I say, "Yes," he seems surprised and delighted.

We go to a table near the back and a waiter appears almost before we sit down. We both order coffee; I also get a piece of banana bread and Tanner just sticks with the coffee.

"I'm really glad you called," he says, which I already knew.

"Why is that?"

"Because there is no way that Ryan did this. It's just not possible."

"Why do you say that?"

"Because I know him."

That's not the answer I was hoping for. His saying that means he's at best a character witness, and if there is anything less important than a character witness in a case where the forensics scream *mass murderer,* I'm hard-pressed to think of what that might be.

"Okay, good to hear. Tell me what you know about Ryan's relationship with the people that were killed, especially Stephen Pearson."

"That was a strange one. They were really close; Ryan was probably Stephen's best friend in the company . . . along with Willie Tirico. It wasn't even like boss and employee, you know? I think they went back to high school together. And all of a sudden, boom . . . Ryan was out of there."

"What do you do there?"

"Right now nothing. I'm a driver, but I'm on disability. I had back surgery two weeks ago. I was one of the moving van drivers . . . a bad back doesn't fit in well with that."

"Sorry to hear that. Different drivers did different things?"

"Yes, we had to bring in a bunch of new drivers when business picked up, so I guess it became logical to give us specialties."

"When are you going back to work?"

"I'm going into the office this week. I figure they'll need all hands on deck."

"Who is running the company now, with Pearson gone?"

"I haven't been there, but I'm sure it must be Mike Shaffer.

He's the controller, and he's been Pearson's right hand all along. And I wouldn't be surprised if Pearson's wife was involved; I guess she owns the place now. I don't envy either of them."

"Why is that?"

He suddenly hesitates to answer and seems guarded, which is a noticeable switch in attitude and demeanor. "It doesn't matter. It's a tough job."

"Eric, I'm going to be straight with you. I need to know everything I can about this entire situation; it's the only way I can effectively represent Ryan. And I can guarantee that I will never reveal that you told me about anything to anyone. That guarantee is absolute.

"So if there's anything else you know, even if you don't necessarily see how it could be helpful to Ryan, you should tell me."

He thinks for a moment and then nods. "Okay. A while back, I would say about two years ago, the company was having problems. It was before they added the private moving and the refrigerated trucks to the business. But it was an open secret that there were money troubles."

"And then?"

"And then all of a sudden they went away. There were rumors that layoffs were about to happen, but they never did. It was like somebody flipped a switch."

"Why was that?"

"The rumor was that someone put a lot of money into the company. And then all of a sudden, things got really secretive, you know? Stephen was always so open about everything, but that changed. And this strange guy started showing up and meeting with him in his office, with the door closed."

"Who was it?"

"I don't know, and nobody else did either. People would

talk about it, but if anybody found out, I never heard about it."

"Would you recognize him if you saw him again?"

"Definitely."

"Okay, if you are able to get a name, it could be helpful to Ryan."

"Not sure I'll be able to."

I don't want to ask Tanner more questions about this stranger because I don't want to spook him. I can always come back to him later.

"Okay, thanks. Tell me what you know about Ryan's relationship with the other victims."

Tanner seems relieved that the subject has been switched. "I don't think it was anything unusual. He knew Denise Clemons, of course, she was in the office all the time. She and Stephen worked closely together. But if Ryan had a lot to do with her, I'm not aware of it."

"What about Donald Muncy?"

"Don? I'm sure Ryan liked him; everybody did. But I don't think they were friends outside the office or anything."

"Can I come back to you with more questions if I have them?"

"Of course . . . of course. And tell Ryan I'm rooting for him and thinking about him, okay?"

"Absolutely."

I'm really getting into this dog-walking thing.

I find I can think clearly while I'm doing it, and it's extremely relaxing. It must be because of the dogs; the chance that I would go for a stroll without them is close to absolute zero.

Maybe it's watching them. They seem to delight in everything; each smell is like a new, wonderful experience. And when unexpected events happen, like a squirrel spotting, their joy is overwhelming.

Our neighborhood is upscale suburbia; and the lawns and gardens define *manicured*. I think if I failed to completely pick up every "deposit" that Tara and Sonny make, I would immediately be reported to the shit police and arrested. So I never leave the house without a plastic bag.

Strangely enough, Tara and Sonny don't seem particularly close. They each do their own thing, both on the walk and at home. They're not mean or aggressive with each other; they just don't seem like close buddies. Each of them clearly prefers human contact.

We're on our morning walk now, which gives me time to think about the case without interruption, other than for occasionally using the aforementioned plastic bag. That's really not my favorite part of the walking experience.

Right now it feels like I have a huge investigative mountain to climb. If Ryan is guilty, then I'm going to climb that mountain and wind up on the other side with nothing to show for it.

If he's not guilty, then I am somehow going to have to dig deep into the mountain and find evidence to prove it.

Of course, if Ryan didn't plant that bomb, then someone else did. Starting out, I have absolutely no idea who that could be, but that has to be the target at the top of the mountain.

I realize I am beating the mountain metaphor to death, but it's hard not to focus on it because I am way better at dog walking than mountain climbing.

Things are going quite well between Nicole and me; I think we're both making an effort. Her reaction to the presence of the dogs remains stunning; I think she likes having them around. I often see her slipping them biscuits and petting them. They seem to like her as well, and dogs are good judges of people.

I'm not sure how well it will go when Nicole realizes how much of my time and focus this case is going to take. I've warned her about it, but she's thinking about my cases as a prosecutor. Things are about to become very different.

And speaking of different, I head home to shower, dress, and leave for a meeting that is going to be very different. It's the exact opposite of all my past experiences.

The meeting is with Karen Vincent, and when I show up at her office, I am greeted warmly by everyone. Karen is the prosecutor on the Ryan Tierney case, and all the people here are my friends and were, until a few months ago, my coworkers.

Karen and I didn't have much of a relationship, mainly because she only arrived about six months before I left. She moved up from Florida because her husband got a big corporate job offer up here, and she brought with her a reputation as a killer in the courtroom.

I'm here because Karen invited me in to discuss the case, no doubt to dangle a plea bargain offer. It will go nowhere because in a case of this magnitude her hands will be tied. Multiple murderers don't get deals worth taking.

Once we're seated, she says, "This is the first case you took?" Her level of incredulousness is annoying.

"I fight injustice wherever I find it. That's just who I am."

"You've read the discovery, right? You see this as an injustice?"

"Not only that, but that's how the jury will see it."

"Right," she says. "Which brings us to the point of the meeting. Life without parole."

"That's your offer? What's the worst he can get if we go to trial and lose?" I ask, already knowing the answer.

"Life without parole." Then, "You know the drill, Andy. We'd always like to avoid a trial when we can, and maybe your client does as well. It can be tough to go through."

"On behalf of my client, we appreciate your concern. But we'll decline your generous offer, appealing as it may be."

"You really want to start out with a loss in a high-profile case?"

"Has the fat lady already sung and I missed it?"

She smiles. "I knew you wouldn't take the offer, and I will admit I'm glad. In this kind of case, the public will want to see the justice system in action, and they should."

"Then you got your wish."

"Okay, then we're agreed, and the offer expires with the conclusion of this sentence."

I smile. "See you in court, Counselor."

aurie Collins said she would meet me at my office; maybe she didn't want to be seen with a defense attorney in public.

She shows up five minutes early, just about as I am realizing I have nothing to offer any visitors in the way of food or drink.

"Andy, nice to see you again," she says, while looking around at the pathetic surroundings.

"I haven't had a chance to fix the place up yet."

She nods. "Clearly."

"Are you hungry? I have all kinds of fruit, downstairs at the fruit stand. Maybe you'd like a cantaloupe?"

The door opens and Sam Willis comes in without knocking. "Oh," he says, when he sees Laurie. "I didn't realize . . ."

"It's okay," I say. "Laurie Collins, this is Sam Willis, my butler. He'd be happy to get you that cantaloupe."

She laughs a great laugh. "That's okay. Hello, Sam."

Sam mutters his hello and then leaves.

"So why am I here?" Laurie asks.

"Because Pete Stanton said there was a chance I could hire you as my investigator."

"To work on the Ryan Tierney case?"

"That's the first one, yes."

She looks troubled, so I say, "You seem less than enthusiastic."

She nods. "I'm considerably less than enthusiastic, but this is the situation I find myself in. I've spent my working life trying to put guilty people away, not trying to get them off."

"If you don't mind my saying so, that's not how you should have been spending your time."

"Excuse me?"

"You should have been trying to find out who was guilty, then if you were right, the system could put them away."

"I don't see the distinction."

"I do. In fact your old job and my new job are exactly the same. We are both trying to determine who actually committed the crime in question."

She frowns. "Innocent until proven guilty."

"It's not just a slogan. It's the way it works. If I were you, and in a way I am, I would get at least as much satisfaction out of making sure the innocent go free as I would in seeing the guilty put away."

"I'm being lectured. I'm not a big fan of being lectured."

"Sorry. Just trying to defend my job, I guess." Then, "It's been an adjustment for me too."

"But your job is to get people off even if they're guilty."

"Fortunately, my job doesn't include making that decision. And yours certainly wouldn't. If you choose to work with me, your job will be to find out the facts . . . end of story. That is all I would ever ask you to do, I can promise you that. The other promise I can make is that I will never take what you find out and lie about it."

She thinks for a while. Then, "You know, I once went to a seminar that your father spoke at. Back when I wanted to be a lawyer."

I smile. "And he talked you out of it?"

"No, lack of money for tuition talked me out of it. But the reason I mention it is that you sound a lot like him." She laughs. "A lot of ideological bullshit."

I return the laugh. "The lawyer doesn't fall far from the tree."

"He was actually pretty inspiring."

"Then maybe it does fall far from the tree."

"Okay," she says. "I'll try it. How much are you going to pay me?"

"I have no idea, but I'll find out. I think the public defender has a reasonably healthy budget for outside investigators."

"So when do we start?"

"How about we meet here tomorrow afternoon at two o'clock? I have a meeting in the morning. What do you want me to have here for you to drink?"

She looks around. "Maybe get yourself a coffee machine."

"Okay. Maybe one that also makes lattes and espresso?"

"Coffee will be fine."

She leaves and Sam comes in a few seconds later; he must have been watching to see her go. "Who was that?"

"My new investigator."

"She looks nothing like Columbo."

"Very true."

"Anyway, you had said you wanted to talk to me?"

"Yes, Sam, you're an accountant. . . ."

"I'm aware of that."

"If a company suddenly gets an infusion of cash, is there any way to find out where it came from?"

"A public company?"

"No, privately owned."

"Then there's no public way to find out, unless they

voluntarily reveal it. Sometimes they'd consider it to their benefit to do so."

"When would that be?"

"One example would be if some savvy investor, say, a Warren Buffett type, took a position in a company. That company would want people to know that because it would make them look good and appealing to other potential investors."

"You said there is 'no public way' to find out who invested? Is there a private way?"

"Sometimes. Let me see what I can find out."

I'm not sure what he's talking about, but I'll take any help I can get.

"Okay," I say. "We're talking about Pearson Trucking."

"Got it. Give me until tomorrow."

Andy, I need to ask you something. You're not going to like it."

Nicole says this as soon as I walk in the door. I'm not sure why she predicts my reaction like that; does she think it will soften the blow when I actually hear it? Maybe she believes that I'll start dreading what she's going to ask to the point that when I finally hear it, it won't sound so bad?

"Then there's still time for you not to ask it," I say.

"I'm afraid I have to. There's a dinner tonight; my parents were supposed to go but Daddy is stuck in Washington. He just called and asked us to fill in for him."

"Any chance it's at Charlie's Sports Bar?"

"Afraid not."

Nicole gives me the rest of the bad news. It's a charity dinner at a fancy hotel in Manhattan. She says I just have time to walk the dogs, shower, and put on my tuxedo.

"Tuxedo? Did I hear that correctly?"

"I'm afraid so. I'm sorry, Andy, but I couldn't say no. I hope you can't either."

The fact is that I could say no, but I won't. This is part of being married; concessions are written right into the rule book. "Sounds great. I was in the mood to wear my tux anyway; even if we were staying home."

So it's off to walk the dogs, and within ninety minutes we

are valet parking in front of the hotel. I'm sure the cost of doing so is expensive to the point that they might as well just keep the car.

When we get inside, I expect a big ballroom full of people, but that's not what we find. Instead the charity has taken over the hotel restaurant, and there are only about seventy guests here. I sincerely doubt that any of them could be described as impoverished peasants.

The menu is all in French, with no translations. We're at a table with six other people, none of whom I know, but I can tell who I am going to talk to all night. The guy next to me, who says his name is Robby Divine, is wearing a tuxedo, and sneakers . . . and a Chicago Cubs hat.

The waiter comes over and says, "What are we sipping tonight?"

Robby says, "I'm 'sipping' a beer . . . out of a bottle."

The evening doesn't turn out nearly as bad as I expected, mainly because Robby and I talk sports the whole time. He also hates these kinds of events, which he is quite willing to point out to everyone.

My kind of guy.

When we leave, he suggests we stay in touch, and he hands me his card. All it says is ROBBY DIVINE, with a phone number.

Once we're in the car, I ask Nicole if she knows anything about him.

"You don't know?" she asks.

"No."

She smiles, I guess at my ignorance. "He is one of the richest men in the world. Pretty much everything you eat, or drive, or wear, he owns a large piece of the company that makes it."

"I guess when you're that rich, you can wear a baseball cap to dinner."

"You seemed like you had a nice time tonight," Nicole says, clearly surprised.

I nod. "I'm a social animal."

"I've heard that about you. Thanks for coming tonight, Andy. I really appreciate it."

"No problem."

"And I know you're going to be very busy with your work. I'll try to respect that."

"Thank you."

"I read some about your case online. I hope your client didn't do it, but the media makes it sound like he did."

"They always think that anyone arrested must be guilty. It wouldn't matter, except the people who will eventually make up the jury are seeing what you're seeing."

"But defendants usually are guilty, aren't they?"

I nod. "More often than not."

"I hope this time they're wrong."

"Me too."

'm not really surprised that Mike Shaffer, the controller of Pearson Trucking, was willing to meet with me.

It's counterintuitive; I am representing the guy that he no doubt believes killed his colleague and boss. One would think he would not want to help me in any way.

And I'm sure he doesn't, but he wouldn't see how a conversation with me will help my cause at all. On the other hand, he'll want to learn whatever he can about the enemy, and he'll think I might reveal something significant.

There is no chance of that. For one thing, I'm not that dumb. More importantly, I don't know anything significant.

When I walk into the offices, I see about ten people either milling about or sitting at their desks. One of them is Eric Tanner, who does not acknowledge me in any way. He clearly doesn't want anyone to know that he has spoken with me, and I can't blame him for that.

There are three offices along the back side of the building, with glass walls allowing the inhabitants to look out into what I would describe as a bullpen area. Of course, it also allows anyone out there to look in.

Two of the offices are empty, and the third has a man who stands and comes to the door. He signals to me to come over, so I have to assume this is Michael Shaffer.

"Mr. Carpenter?"

"Andy."

"Come on in, Andy. Mike Shaffer." He shakes my hand as I enter the office, then goes back behind his desk while I take a chair across from him.

"So, what can I do for you?"

"As I said on the phone, I'm representing Ryan Tierney."

"How is Ryan?"

"Innocent."

Shaffer smiles. "I would expect you to say nothing else."

"Glad I could justify your confidence. You know Ryan well?"

"Of course. We're a small company; everybody knows everybody. I've always thought highly of Ryan, and I must say that Stephen Pearson did as well."

"Yet he fired him."

"He did, yes."

"Why?"

"I assume you've done your homework, so I think you probably know that already, but I don't think I'm going to comment. Let's just say that in business some decisions have to be made, unpleasant or not."

"So you'll be taking over?"

"I see it as being on an interim basis, subject to Anna's decisions."

"Anna?"

"Stephen's wife; she is now the sole owner."

"So the people who injected money into the company a couple of years ago don't have an ownership interest?"

I said it to get a reaction, to see if Eric Tanner was right about the cash infusion, and I get one. First silence, and then a curt "I don't know what you're talking about."

"You're the controller and you don't know anything about

a lot of money coming into the company? At a time when it was in trouble? Were you out that day?"

"I think we're done here. If you've come to make accusations . . ."

"You think that pointing out that a company has an investor is an accusation?"

"Mr. Carpenter . . ."

"Did Stephen Pearson have any enemies that you know of?"

"Which part of 'I think we're done here' did you not understand?"

"So you'd rather answer these questions on the witness stand, under oath?"

"Good-bye, Mr. Carpenter."

I stand up. "By the way, I can't believe you didn't offer me anything to eat or drink. I always offer my guests a cantaloupe. It's common courtesy."

I leave, and on my way out Eric Tanner again does not acknowledge me. Shaffer badly overreacted to my comment about the cash infusion. He could have just smiled and shrugged it off, but he didn't.

People generally do that for a reason.

Laurie Collins arrived early for our two o'clock meeting. I know that because when I arrive, she is already sitting in my office, munching on a peach. She obviously made a stop downstairs before coming up.

"How did you get in?" I ask, since I know I locked the door. The discovery documents are here, and I would not want them stolen or tampered with.

"Sam let me in. He said you should come by later; he has something to tell you."

"Good peaches, huh?"

"Excellent; I put this one on your tab. And she has maybe the best-looking broccoli and brussels sprouts I've ever seen."

"I wouldn't know."

"You don't eat them?"

"Not even if you fried them and then covered them in chocolate sauce."

She laughs. Then, "Okay, boss, what's my assignment?"

"First let's talk about the case." I lay out everything I know, including the basics of what is in the discovery. When I'm finished, I'm surprised to see that I've talked for forty-five minutes, and she has not interrupted once.

She finally asks, "Can I read through the discovery?"

"Of course, but I only have the one copy, so please do so here. I'll get a coffee machine; I promise."

"So what do you want me to do?"

"Let's talk about how we will operate. I'll give you assignments when something comes up that I need you to do. But just as important is for you to conduct the investigation in the way your instincts tell you. You know more about this stuff than I do."

"Okay."

"But please keep me informed at all times about what you're doing. I don't want us working at cross-purposes. And obviously I want to know things as you learn them."

"Fair enough."

"For now, I would focus on the victims. If our boy didn't kill them, then someone else did. It would be nice to find out a likely candidate for that."

"Okay. With a focus on Stephen Pearson?"

"Yes, but not exclusively. It's hard to see someone else as the target since it was Pearson's car. The killer would have had no way of knowing other people would be in it. But I don't believe in dismissing a possibility before it's checked out."

"Agreed. You mind if I hang around and go through the discovery now?"

"Not at all." Then, "Are you coming to terms with working on this side of the aisle?"

She smiles. "It's a process. If I find I can't do it, then I'll quit and figure out something else to do. But it won't be before this case is resolved; I won't leave you hanging."

"Thank you. Now I'm going to go find out what Sam wants."

S am is on his computer when I enter his office. Sam is always on his computer.

He has quite a setup, with three screens side by side. Right now he is only working with the center one; I know that because the other two show screen savers.

"Hey, Andy . . . I'll be right with you."

He does some more typing for maybe a minute, then stops and turns to me. "I've been looking into that thing with Pearson Trucking."

For a moment I forgot that I had talked to him about it. Once he said that a private company didn't have to report their financial information, I had thought his saying that he would look into it wouldn't get anywhere.

"And?"

"Interesting stuff; at least I think so."

"Good. Let's hear it."

"The company was in significant difficulty starting about two years ago. A couple of times they barely made payroll."

"How do you know this?"

"I'll get to that. . . . Let me finish first. They received a cash infusion back then of seven hundred and fifty thousand dollars. Since then there have been three additional infusions of approximately a half million each time.

"I wouldn't describe the last million as essential; the company has gotten back on its feet pretty well."

"So if they said they fired Ryan Tierney for financial reasons that wouldn't be true?"

"It certainly wasn't necessary from what I can see," Sam says.

"Who put in the cash?"

"I have no idea. Untraceable wire transfers."

"Has the company paid back the money?"

"There is no evidence of that at all. Maybe the investors took an equity position in the company, but there is no evidence of that either."

"How do you know all this?" I ask, though I've pretty much figured out the answer.

"Let's just say that their cybersecurity leaves something to be desired."

"You hacked into their system?"

"That's an ugly word, but yes. There was no other way to get the information."

"That's illegal, Sam."

"They can't trace anything back to me, Andy. I'm really good at this."

"Illegality exists on its own. It's not dependent on the perpetrator being caught."

"I take it you would rather I had not done it?"

"Yes," I say, though that is not entirely true. I am quite happy to have the information.

"Okay, I hear you. Won't happen again."

"Good. But I do appreciate your trying to help."

It's a sign of my lack of progress that my main source of information is my client.

If he knew anything truly valuable and helpful, he wouldn't be my client; he'd be going to bars and Mets games.

But I'm back at the jail talking to him because it's better than being back at the office talking to myself.

"Were you aware that a while back Pearson Trucking was in financial trouble?"

He nods. "Everyone was."

"What got them out of it?"

"I don't know; maybe Stephen put some of his own money into it. But they were talking about layoffs and maybe having to close up, and then all of a sudden they were back on their feet."

"Did adding private moving help?"

"I would assume so, but it would have helped more if they didn't do it ass-backwards."

"What do you mean?"

"It wasn't just the private moving end; the company was just really inefficient."

"How so?"

"The way they utilized their resources. I should say the way I utilized them; I was sort of the dispatcher."

"So why did you do it that way?"

"Because every time I tried to institute new procedures, I got shot down. Just like when I tried to push better safety procedures on the food."

"Why?"

He shrugs. "They had different ideas, I guess. I kept trying, until finally I was ready to give up."

"Give me an example of their inefficient way of doing things."

"Okay, let's say we got a call that a family was moving from New Jersey to Billings, Montana, and they wanted us to move them. So we'd take the job and in the process the huge truck necessary would go there and back. With the unloading, he might be gone for five days. We're also talking about a driver and a helper."

"So?"

"So we could not charge them enough to make that worthwhile."

"So you should have turned down the job?"

"That wouldn't have been such a terrible idea, but there was a better way. Make an effort to find cargo that needed to come East; that way the truck wouldn't be coming back empty for no money. We'd profit both ways."

"Seems to make sense."

He frowns. "Tell me about it."

"Who did you complain to?"

"Mostly Mike Shaffer."

"The controller? Why him?"

"I reported to him. He was much more than a controller; he was Stephen's go-to guy for pretty much everything. Stephen just stayed in his office and pretended to be busy; Mike did all the real work."

"Do you think he'll take over permanently?"

Tierney shrugs. "It will be up to Anna, Stephen's wife."

"Has she been active in the business?"

"No, but they were very close, and she's smart. They would discuss everything; Stephen always told me how much he valued her input."

"I was told that Pearson would get visitors in his office that no one knew, and he was secretive about it. You know anything about that?"

"I heard the same thing, but I never saw anyone."

"Okay."

"How's it going? Are we making progress?"

"It's early and it's a process, Ryan. All I can say is I know it's rough, but hang in there."

I'm a little surprised when Robby Divine takes the call.

"Robby, it's Andy Carpenter," I say, although he would know that because his assistant would have told him when she put through the call. "We met at the dinner the other night and— . . ."

"Did I give you the impression we were therefore buddies?"

"I thought we shared a special, intimate moment."

He laughs, which I am glad to hear. Then, "Did you get the flowers I sent?"

"They're beautiful. That's one of the reasons I called."

"Uh-oh. What's the other one? What's the charity, and how much is it going to cost me?"

"Not a dime. By the way, Ernie Banks."

"What about him?"

"Nothing; I just thought it would put you in a good, favor-doing mood to hear his name, Mr. Cub."

"Didn't work. Get to the point."

"I googled you. You own a company called Summit Freight Lines."

"I was already aware of that."

"I want to talk to someone there. Someone who really knows the trucking business."

"That's the favor?"

"That's it."

"Call Paul Holt in the morning, after ten. He's at the main office in Rutherford."

"What does he do?"

"Not enough, which I tell him all the time. But he's the CEO."

"I appreciate this. And may I say, you were a charming dinner companion."

"And may I say, you're a pain in the ass."

"You may."

"You're a pain in the ass."

Paul Holt was rather responsive to the call he must have gotten from Robby Divine.

When I called him this morning and requested a meeting, he said, "Come on over. I've got time now." I got the feeling he would have made time even if he were heading to his own wedding ceremony.

I was scheduled to meet in my office with Laurie Collins this morning, so I called her and pushed that meeting back a few hours.

Rutherford is only fifteen minutes from Paterson, so within a half hour of my making the phone call, I'm sitting across from Holt in his office.

"I had the pleasure of meeting your father at a charity dinner a number of years ago," he says.

"I met Robby the same way."

"Was he wearing his Cubs hat?"

I nod. "Proudly."

"No matter how much they lose, he sticks with them. He's either loyal or nuts."

"Or both."

"So what can I do for you?"

"I'm representing the man accused of killing Stephen Pearson and two other people."

He nods sadly. "I knew Stephen rather well. I liked him."

"Do you know much about his company?"

"Some . . . not too much. We're a much larger business than they are, so we would not consider them direct competition."

"They wouldn't pursue the same clients or jobs that you would?"

"Let me rephrase it a bit. Yes, trucking is basically a zero-sum game. If they are hauling a load, then we aren't hauling that same load. But our clients are basically bigger and steadier; we have established long relationships. So we're not out there chasing the kind of business that Stephen was; we don't need to be."

"I see."

"And once they went into personal relocation . . . a traditional moving business . . . well, we're not in that at all. Same with trucking the food and groceries."

"You don't handle food?"

"We do, but we do it for established American companies that have their infrastructure here. Pearson, and a couple of other companies, found a niche handling mostly imported foods; they essentially became their American distribution operation."

"Not enough money in that part of it for you?"

"Not enough to change our business model," Holt says. "We focus on what we do best."

"Were you aware that Pearson was in trouble a couple of years ago?"

"I was, though it wasn't top of mind for me. I believe it was common knowledge. At one point Stephen even spoke vaguely to me about a merger, which would have essentially meant our buying his company."

"You weren't interested?"

"We ultimately would not have been, even though we could

have gotten it on the cheap. But it didn't matter because Stephen backed off. I assumed he got outside financing."

"There is a school of thought that the financing came from less than reputable channels." I'm guessing at that based on Sam's information and Shaffer's reaction when I asked him about it.

Holt nods. "Always possible in this business."

"But you don't know who might have supplied it?"

"I'm afraid I don't."

"No potential names?" I ask.

"Not really; it's fortunately not a world we need to inhabit. We are well financed."

"Robby."

He nods. "Robby. Beneath that Cubs hat lies very significant financial resources."

"Whoever supplied the money to Pearson, assuming it wasn't a bank, what would be their motivation?"

"Usually to get back their investment plus exorbitant interest. Failing that they could disband the company and sell off the pieces. Stephen could have felt tremendous pressure to get out from under. Taking money from those people is essentially a delaying action and almost always intensifies the crisis over time."

"So in the two scenarios you're presenting, Pearson would have been paying back the money at high interest or would have been forced to give an equity position?"

"Yes."

I don't bother telling him that Sam's illegal computer work showed neither of those things happening.

"Thanks for your time," I say.

He smiles. "Any friend of Robby's . . ."

head back to my office to meet with Laurie.

On the way I process what I learned from Paul Holt, which is easy to do because I learned very little.

Basically it was confirmation of what I already knew: Pearson Trucking had been in trouble, and then suddenly they were not. I have no doubt they got a cash infusion, and that it wasn't exactly from Goldman Sachs.

Underlying all of this is that even if I knew the details, I have no reason or ability to tie it in to the car bombing. Not that I have to prove to the jury that it's related, but I do have to show them that it could be and that the people who lent the money were violent enough to have done this.

Could it be as simple as Pearson reneging on the debt? That his business turned around but he wasn't making the payments he was supposed to make?

That seems like a bit of an overreaction; it would make more sense to threaten Pearson, or even to do something to him on a much smaller scale. When a person is blown up in a car, it then becomes tough to ask him to make future payments on a loan.

I get to the office about fifteen minutes before Laurie is supposed to be here. I stop at the fruit stand to drop off my rent check with Sofia Hernandez. I also get some Jersey tomatoes, which are huge and incredibly juicy. Nicole loves them, so if I give them to her, she might forgive me for upending our lives so I can defend a possible mass murderer.

I live in hope.

I go to open the door to my office only to find that it's already open. My hope that Sam is the reason for that is dashed when I see a rather large and ugly individual sitting at my desk. His face is fleshy and somewhat misshapen; it looks like a hunk of dough as it's just starting to be flattened into a pizza crust.

The intruder looks comfortable, like he doesn't have a care in the world. He wasn't surprised by my showing up; he was anticipating it.

"Come on in, asshole" is his greeting. Since there is no one else here, I must be the asshole he's referring to.

I walk in a few feet, leaving myself the ability to get out if I have to, and I'm afraid I'm going to have to. "Who the hell are you?"

He shakes his head. "Doesn't matter; if you're smart, you'll never see me again. You're smart, aren't you, lawyer?"

I'm scared, but his message strangely calms me a bit. It doesn't sound like he's here to hurt or kill me, but rather to deliver a message.

"Say what you want to say and then get out of my office," I say, pretending to be tough and unafraid, neither of which is close to true.

He stands up and starts walking toward me from the left, and I stupidly move to the right to keep my distance. Suddenly I realize that if he's at all quick, he can block my exit.

"Be careful, asshole. I have permission to break your arm . . . maybe even both of them."

I don't say anything; I just wait for the message to be delivered.

"Stop messing with Pearson Trucking; it has nothing to do with your case."

"I'll be the judge of that." I have no idea why I said that; maybe there is a courageous idiot somewhere inside me.

"Yeah?" he says, unintimidated. "Maybe the arm-breaking idea is a good one."

He takes one step toward me and then I hear, "I don't think so."

We both look and there in the open doorway is Laurie, a gun in her hand pointing at the intruder. "Put your fat ass in that chair," she says, and I think she means him, because my ass is normal size, maybe even petite.

He looks at her for a moment and apparently decides she is serious and in charge. As he walks to the desk, he says, "You are making a big mistake."

"We'll see about that, dipshit."

She takes out her phone with one hand while holding the gun on him with the other. After a few moments, she says, "Tom, I've got an intruder here; I need you to send a couple of your people to make the arrest." She then gives our location.

"What are you doing?" the guy asks when she hangs up.

"You can't figure it out? You really are as dumb as you look."

"You're messing with the wrong people."

"Really? Which people are that? Who sent you? Because you're too stupid to find this place with a GPS."

"I got nothing more to say to you."

So none of us say anything for the next five minutes, at which point we start to hear sirens. Within moments four cops are in my office, and Laurie is telling them the situation.

They cuff the guy and take him out to their car. I'm still rather stunned by the entire episode.

"You okay?" Laurie asks, after they've left.

"Fine; I was just about to beat the shit out of him when you walked in."

She laughs. "I know. I intervened so he wouldn't get hurt." Then, "I want to go down to the station and make sure this is handled right. He trespassed and threatened to break your arm; he needs to sit in a cell."

"How long will you be?"

"Maybe an hour and a half."

"Can we meet at my house? I don't feel like sitting here."

"Sure."

"And thank you for what you did. You were amazing."

She smiles. "Just another day at the office." She looks around. "An office that is still without a coffee machine."

I give her the address and she leaves. At this point I'm thinking Laurie Collins was a good hire.

Nicole, this is Laurie Collins. Laurie . . . Nicole Gant."
They greet each other nicely, and Nicole asks if she
can get Laurie something to eat or drink. Laurie thanks her,
but passes on the offer.

"I'll leave you two alone to work," Nicole says, smiling.

I have no idea what Nicole is thinking. I try to imagine
how I would feel if she brought George Clooney or Brad Pitt
home; I think I'd be okay with it, but maybe not.

Hopefully she trusts me, or maybe she doesn't trust me but
feels secure in the fact that I wouldn't have a chance with Laurie if I wanted to. Either way, Nicole is not acting as if there's
a problem, so there's nothing for me to do.

Laurie and I go into the den to talk about the case and the
incident in my office. I haven't told Nicole about it because
she would just worry, and because she is already upset about
the world I am living and working in.

It's an ethical dilemma that I am going to have to confront,
because the truth is that if someone can break into my office,
they can break into this house. Nicole has a right to know
that.

"How did it go at the station?" I ask.

"Fine. Your visitor was booked and locked up. His name is
Victor Cobb."

"What do we know about him?"

"Well, for one thing, he's spent almost half of his adult life in prison; they installed a revolving door and named it after him. Most of the charges were for assault; a couple were for drug possession with intent to distribute."

"Who does he work for? I'm assuming he was sent to the office and didn't come up with the idea on his own."

"I'm sure that's true. But Victor's sort of a hired gun." Laurie sees my reaction and qualifies it. "That's just an expression I'm using as none of the convictions were for the use of a firearm. But there is no consistent employer on his rap sheet, and he is certainly not talking. Somebody needed an asshole to threaten you, and Victor was a logical choice."

"So what will happen to him?"

"As long as you will testify to criminal trespassing and threatened bodily harm, he'll probably go away again, based on his past record. But I would assume bail will be set, so in the short term he could be back on the street."

"Super."

"Victor won't be your problem. He's already screwed up, so whoever hired him could certainly choose to send someone better, maybe a lot better."

"Double super."

She shakes her head. "Unlikely it would be now. As bad as it went for poor Victor, he did deliver the message. Now they will wait to see how you react."

"I'll react by continuing to do whatever the hell I'm doing."

"What would have made them think you were causing them trouble?"

"Only two possibilities. I asked the controller, Mike Shaffer, about the cash infusion, and he did not react well to it.

He's the most likely candidate to have told somebody about it, and that resulted in Victor's visit. The only other thing was that Sam was poking around on the internet, but he assures me that no one could trace that."

"I don't know enough about the internet to know what 'poking around' means, and I'm not particularly anxious to be educated about it," she says.

"For now I guess you should poke around yourself, outside the internet. It would be helpful to know whatever we can learn about the money that turned Pearson's business around."

"You have any concrete reason to connect it to the murders?"

"No, but it's slightly suspicious, because of Shaffer's reaction and because the money was sent by untraceable wires. Those things make it more promising than anything else I have. And it seems to have provoked people with a tendency towards violence."

"Okay. Anything else you want me to do?"

"Yes. See if you can get me in to see Pearson's widow. Her name is Anna."

"Why me?"

"Women don't generally react well to me in situations like this; I can be a little heavy-handed and insensitive."

She smiles. "Hard to believe." Then, "I'll talk to her, but she may not want to be helpful to the defense team."

"I'm aware."

"By the way, do you have the money to hire a second investigator?"

"I do; the budget for that from the PD's office is surprisingly generous. You have someone in mind?"

She nods. "I do. I'll put him on as an 'as needed' situation. But I think it will be helpful."

"What's his name?"

"Marcus."

"Does he have a last name? Or is that the last name?"

"Marcus Clark."

"I've never heard of him," I say.

"He prefers it that way."

I can't help it: the first thing I notice about Randy Clemons is that he has a prosthetic leg.

I'm at Gilmore's Gym in Garfield, which is where Clemons wanted to meet. There are only three people in the place; 11:00 A.M. must not be prime workout time. I would have no idea about that; I've never had a prime workout time.

But I'm assuming it's Clemons because when he sees me come in, clearly not dressed in workout clothes, he waves to me. He gets off some exercise machine contraption that I would kill myself on if I ever tried to make it work.

He's wearing gym shorts, and one of his legs is made out of thin metal. It doesn't seem to bother him any; he barely has a limp. But I'm finding it hard to stop staring at it.

Clemons is a big guy; he probably has five inches and fifty pounds on me. When we shake hands, mine disappears in his. "Randy Clemons," he says, and I respond cleverly with "Andy Carpenter." We obviously speak each other's language.

"Come on over here."

He leads me to an area where they make and sell smoothies, all of which are filled with so much healthy stuff as to be completely unappealing. If someone would invent a french fry smoothie, they would make a fortune.

He gets some kind of drink; I think I hear "wheat germ"

when he orders it, and then he brings it back to our table and sits down. "You sure you don't want one?" he asks.

"I have rarely been more sure of anything in my life."

"Okay. I assume you want to talk about what happened to Denise; I know you're representing the guy that killed her."

"You left out *allegedly.*"

He frowns. "Yeah, I know. That's probably my least favorite word, but I know the drill. You know I used to be a cop?"

"Yes."

He points to his metal leg. "Line of duty; permanent disability. There's not a day I don't wish I was back on the job. And I could still do it if they'd let me."

"Sorry about that."

"Yeah. So I said I would talk to you because I want to understand how an asshole could do something like he did. I mean, talk about cowardly. . . ."

"Do you think Denise could have been the target?"

"No chance. Why would anyone want to hurt her?"

"I'm good at asking questions; at this point I'm not so good at answering them. So you think the target was Pearson?"

He shrugs. "That seems to be where this is heading, but I really didn't know the guy. It sure as hell wasn't Denise; she did not have an enemy in the world."

"Did she ever say anything to you about Pearson which might shed some light on this? Maybe some problem he was having, or some potential enemy? I admit I'm fishing here."

"Yeah, you sure are."

"There were people that loaned him a lot of money when the business was in trouble. Did Denise ever mention that?"

"No."

"And Pearson would have visitors that he was secretive about. I know Denise sat right outside his office."

"Who you trying to pin this on?" he asks, clearly getting angry.

"I'm trying to pin it on whoever did this crime."

"Let me ask you something. You have any idea what it's like to get woken up by a phone call in the morning to tell you that your wife is dead? That they couldn't even identify her body, but they're sure it's her?"

"No, I—"

He cuts me off. "I loved my wife; she knew nothing about any of the crap you're talking about and she did not deserve to die."

"I'm not saying—"

He cuts me off again; this has become a one-way conversation. "Here's what I'm saying. If you get this guy off, maybe on some bullshit technicality, I'm going to shoot him in the face and watch him die. That clear enough?"

"I'm getting the gist of it." I stand up. "Enjoy your wheat germ."

When I get to the car, before I drive off, I check the emails on my phone. There is one from an address that I don't recognize. The subject line is *This is the guy.*

I open it and there is a photo of a man apparently leaving Mike Shaffer's office. It was obviously secretly taken and then sent to me by Eric Tanner. I don't recognize the guy, but I am sure as hell going to find out who he is.

forward the emailed photo to Laurie.

Eric Tanner must have taken it surreptitiously, which took a lot of guts. There is always the chance that Laurie could recognize him, but much more likely is the chance that she can find out who he is from her former police colleagues.

Of course, there is no guarantee that he has criminal connections of any kind. He could be someone there to replace the drapes in the office, or to discuss some perfectly legal and aboveboard business issue.

I'm going to head home to walk the dogs and then have dinner, but first I stop at the jail to show the photo to Ryan in case he has seen the guy in the office.

Unfortunately, he shows no hint of recognition. He says he's good with faces and is quite sure he's never seen this one. But while that is no help, at least I got another fun trip to the jail out of it.

Tara and Sonny greet me at the door with tails wagging. Nicole comes out of the kitchen, a smile on her face, but nowhere near as happy as the two dogs. She tells me that dinner will be ready in a half hour, so I quickly grab the leashes and we head off.

Once again I am struck by how simple and uncomplicated things are for Tara and Sonny, and they seem totally fine with it. No complaints, no jealousies . . . just a view of the world as a happy place filled with promise. I don't know how they got this upbeat attitude, but I'm sure not going to law school has to be a part of it.

During dinner with Nicole I try not to think about the case, which is difficult because in these situations the case becomes all-consuming. I realize in the moment that I have no idea what Nicole did all day today, or yesterday, for that matter.

"How was your day?" I ask, the most marriagey question of all time.

She shrugs. "Uneventful. Did some reading, had lunch with Sandy, and then went to the salon."

Uh-oh. "Yeah, I was just going to say that your hair looks great."

"Thank you, but that would be a coincidence. I had a mani-pedi."

I've never had a mani-pedi in my life; I don't know why anyone would. I guess if you strapped me down and forced me to have one of them, I'd prefer the mani to the pedi. Why bother to make something look good and then stuff it in a pair of socks all day?

But I want to appear interested, so I ask, "Does the mani always come before the pedi? You know, I mean, chronologically?"

She smiles. "Not always." Then, "Are you really interested in this?"

"Not intensely, no."

"I guessed that. So we can't talk about my day because it's boring, and we can't talk about yours because it involves violence and murder. Seems like we have a problem."

"We can overcome it."

"How?"

"Well, for one thing, this case will end, and my next one

won't be about murder. It might be about assault, or arson, or something fun like that. And maybe during your next mani-pedi you'll read about something interesting we can discuss."

She laughs; Nicole has always had a great laugh. "We have a lot to look forward to."

The rest of the evening is pleasant, but I think we both know that she's right . . . we have a problem.

Nicole goes to sleep but I stay up for a while to go over some case documents and think unproductively about the case.

The unannounced and unwelcome visit to my office by Victor Cobb, while scaring the shit out of me, is nonetheless probably a positive. It at least shows me that there are some dangerous people involved in this case who aren't named Ryan Tierney.

If the people that sent Victor are worried that I will un-cover something damaging to them, the logical conclusion to be drawn from that is that there is something damaging to find. Maybe Stephen Pearson was a similar danger to them and died because of it.

Maybe I should start finding someone to start my car for me in the mornings.

I'm meeting Laurie at my office at ten o'clock this morning.

It's a sign of my pathetic cowardliness that I would like her to get there before me, just in case there is another thug like Victor Cobb waiting in ambush.

But I summon up my courage and get here fifteen minutes early because I want to talk to Sam. Sam seems to always be in his office, staring at his computer, and this time is no exception.

"Sam, are you sure you didn't see any examples of Pearson Trucking paying back the loan to whoever provided it?"

He nods. "I'm positive. All the payouts were for equipment, payroll, normal-course-of-business-type things."

"And you couldn't find where the loans were coming from?"

"No. They were untraceable wire transfers."

"What would be the reason for someone to do that?" I ask.

"To send untraceable wire transfers? So they couldn't be traced."

"Might Stephen Pearson have been paying back the money through other means? Maybe from his personal funds? I mean, he is the sole owner of the company."

Sam nods. "Certainly could be. Or he could have another company I don't know about. I could look for all these things, but . . ."

"I know. It's illegal."

"But harmless."

"How is that?"

"Who did I hurt by looking into his company?"

Sam has a point, or at least something I can use for rationalization purposes. Nobody was hurt, at least not that I can see. And anything Sam might uncover I could probably get later through subpoenas authorized by the court. So what he did, or what he could do moving forward, is simply a way of informing me as to what would be worth subpoenaing.

"And there is no chance that what you do can be traced back to you?"

"Zero; like I said, I'm really good at this. And nobody would have incentive to try to trace it anyway. I'm not going in and doing any damage; I'm not changing things in any way, so there is no evidence that I'm even there. All I'm doing is looking around."

This is not an easy call for me. I've been a defense attorney for what feels like twenty minutes, and I'm already directing someone to break the law? I can feel my father staring at me, and not with pride and admiration.

On the other hand, what if I can uncover something that would help an innocent man avoid a life sentence? Isn't that worth a little harmless rule bending?

"Okay, see what you can find out, Sam. But be careful. And you're officially coming on the team as a paid investigator."

"That's not necessary."

"Yes, it is. If anything ever happens, I want you to be able to say you were following your boss's orders."

"Good morning, gentlemen."

It's Laurie's voice, and it almost makes me jump out of my skin. She's standing in the doorway, and I realize in the moment that I hope she didn't hear what we were talking about.

I don't know her that well, but she has been a cop, and by all accounts a damn good, honest one. For all I know she might turn us in for conspiring to commit these illegal computer acts.

That's always the danger when you surround yourself with people of integrity. I do not recommend it.

She continues, "Didn't mean to interrupt, but I heard you talking, and . . ."

"No problem," I say. "We were just finishing up here. Sam has joined the team as a sort of cyber-investigator. A keyboard Columbo."

Sam smiles. "That's me."

She returns the smile. "Welcome aboard."

Laurie and I go back to my office. "Still no coffee machine?"

"No. But I'm working on it; I'm researching different models. It's a big decision."

"Right. It wasn't hard identifying the photo of the guy coming out of Shaffer's office. Two of my ex-colleagues immediately recognized him."

"Hopefully he's not a hit man."

"Nothing like that; but that doesn't mean much in this case."

"Why? Who is he?"

"His name is Kenneth Burks. He is definitely not hired muscle; he would loosely be described as a businessman."

"Why loosely?"

"Because he works for Jason Shore. Ever heard of him?"

"Yes, I think so. Wealthy guy? Does a lot of charity stuff?"

She nods. "That's him. Goes out of his way to appear respectable."

"But he's not?"

"I guess that depends on your definition."

"I'm guessing there's another shoe to drop here."

"Yes. Jason Shore owns, or at least partially owns, a lot of different businesses. It's the way he comes to those businesses that may be what is important to us."

"How does he do that?"

"In stark terms, he's a loan shark. But not the kind who gives people loans until payday, or covers gambling debts, or funds payments to maintain drug habits, all at crazy-high interest. That would be penny-ante stuff to Jason Shore. He works on a much-higher plane."

"What do you mean?"

"People and businesses of high income and value who have run into hard times and can't get a bank to return their calls . . . that's who Shore preys on. But if his 'clients' don't pay up, he doesn't take them to court or force them to declare bankruptcy."

"He scares them into paying?"

"Very much so, or at least he tries to. He is said to have a small army of individuals ready to do his debt collection for him. It has a tendency to get people to pay up. If they do, then he makes a huge profit on the loan. Because those kind of people are not used to dealing with this kind of potential violence; they panic."

"And if they can't pay?"

She shrugs. "Not a problem for Shore. He has it built in to the agreement that he gets an equity position in their company, which soon turns into full or majority ownership."

"So Shore forces them out?"

"If it suits him to do so; sometimes he wants them to stay on, with him in control. And he does it all while retaining his image as Mr. Respectable."

"I like this," I say. "I like this a lot."

Willie Tirico was anxious to talk to me and was willing to come to my office to do it.

Willie is the high school friend of both Stephen Pearson and Ryan Tierney that Pearson also hired. Ryan told me that Willie would be helpful in any way he could.

"We were like the Three Musketeers, but we were way too cool to call ourselves that," Willie says with a smile.

"Understandable," I say.

"In fact, I don't think anybody thought we were cool at all."

Since I don't really care about their high school coolness, I try to steer the conversation elsewhere. "What's the first thing you thought about when you heard about what happened to Stephen and the others that night?"

"The truth is I'm sort of ashamed at the answer to that."

"Why?"

"Well, I was at the party, and I was going to drink a lot and let Stephen drive me home. But then I realized it would be a hassle to get my car in the morning, and I'm really not that big a drinker, so I didn't."

"So?"

"So the first thing I thought about was that it could have been me. I could have been in that car."

"It's an understandable reaction. Before you heard that

Ryan was a suspect, was there anyone you thought of that could have done it?"

"I wish I could come up with someone. But I honestly can't. Stephen wasn't perfect, but I can't see anyone wanting to kill him, and definitely not Ryan."

"What do you mean, he wasn't perfect?"

"I don't really like talking bad about the dead, you know? And for all his faults, Stephen was a great guy. I owe him a lot; he hired me when no one else would. I've built a comfortable life because of him."

"I understand that. But maybe something you say could help find his killer. I would think you'd want that, and I know he would."

Tirico takes a moment, apparently to reflect on the logic of that. "Well, for one thing, Stephen was a gambler. A pretty big one; he'd bet you on anything."

"Did he ever get in too deep?"

"Depends on the definition of *too deep*. I know he lost a lot of money. He kept a bunch of money in the office safe; he used it for different things, but I think one of those things was to pay his gambling debts."

"Was he a gambler in business also?"

"I think so, but I don't know for sure. One thing was true: he wanted to protect his employees. I can tell you that. That was like a badge of honor to him; his people came first."

"Does the name Jason Shore mean anything to you?"

"No. Should it?"

"Doesn't matter. What other flaws did Stephen have?"

"Well . . . he wasn't the most faithful husband."

"He had affairs?"

"Yes, though I don't know the women. He was careful about that. But he confided in me sometimes; he told me it was okay with Anna . . . his wife. She understood and put up with it."

"You know her?"

"Sure. For almost as long as I knew Stephen."

"Could you get her to talk to me?"

"I could try, but I have to be careful. She's my boss now."

"I understand. Will she be involved in running the company?"

He shrugs. "I don't know. She's smart, but running a trucking company isn't exactly a barrel of laughs, you know? Maybe she'll just want to bail out and sell the thing."

"What do you think of Mike Shaffer?"

"Between us?"

"Of course."

"Not much."

"Why do you say that?"

"He doesn't care about people. He cares about the company, and he cares about himself."

"Why would Pearson fire Ryan?"

"I have no idea; I was really upset about it."

"Okay. If you don't mind, can you try and get Anna Pearson to talk to me? Don't jeopardize your job or anything, though."

"I'll do my best. And you do your best to get Ryan out of prison."

"That I can promise you."

Laurie's identification of Kenneth Burks as the man that is visiting Mike Shaffer is a huge development.

I'm betting that Burks is also the guy that was visiting with Stephen Pearson in Pearson's office in the weeks and months before he was killed.

That Burks is the right-hand man of Jason Shore allows me to make a logical assumption, though admittedly without the facts to back it up. That is that Stephen Pearson, when his business was in deep trouble, turned to Shore for the financing enabling it to continue. He probably went to the banks and was turned down. And Shore then came through to the tune of more than $2 million.

Continuing down this logical path, Pearson did not repay the loan, and Shore had him killed. Case closed, and Ryan Tierney and his genius lawyer walk off into the sunset together.

Of course, this analysis is not without its flaws. For one thing, Sam found no evidence of loan repayments at all, despite that Pearson Trucking has mostly thrived since the infusion of cash. And the loan cash kept coming in over time, which is not an indication of Shore's dissatisfaction with the relationship.

The other aspect that doesn't make sense is that Pearson was murdered. Not that Shore is said to be above such a thing, but rather that he seems to have done so precipitously. Murder is not usually a first step in these situations, but if Pearson had any legs or thumbs broken in the weeks and months leading up to his death, I'm not aware of it.

But even if there are answers to those questions, and I can find them, I would still have to connect Shore and the loans to the murders. Maybe there's a straight line. . . . Shore loaned the money, Pearson stiffed him on the repayments, and Shore had Pearson killed. I would still need evidence to even get the theory before a jury, no less to prove it.

Yesterday, when I was walking Tara and Sonny, I spent some time thinking about Ryan Tierney's guilt or innocence. It hit me again how different my perspective has to be as a defense attorney. I'm still not used to it.

As a prosecutor, I never thought about it. I, and the people I represented, were sure the suspect was guilty or we would not have brought charges. Our obligation was only to bring a case that we thought we could prove beyond a reasonable doubt.

As a defense attorney, I obviously have no such assurance of my client's guilt or innocence one way or the other. And the system is structured in such a way that it is not supposed to matter to me. Or, if it does matter, then my view is not supposed to change the way I behave.

I am to zealously represent my client whether or not he committed the crime.

I haven't thought much about Tierney's culpability, maybe because I didn't want to face it one way or the other. But the situation with Shore opens a slight window, and I find myself looking through it.

Actually, it's not even a window . . . it's more like a small slit. But if Pearson made an enemy of Jason Shore, then at least it opens up a theory under which Tierney could be innocent. And I can't help it, but that is important to me.

I head home, stopping first at the pharmacy to buy some

vitamins that Nicole asked me to pick up, as well as a coffee machine. Once I buy the machine, I'll have to figure out how to work it, but maybe Sam or Laurie can help with that. I'm not great with mechanical stuff.

Unfortunately, it turns out they don't sell coffee machines and the vitamins are locked behind some fiberglass barrier. It takes me five minutes to get someone with a key to come over.

"You have a lot of vitamin thefts?" I ask.

"We have all kinds of thefts," he says, as he hands me the bottle of vitamins.

"Let me ask you a question. If they weren't locked up, you're afraid someone like me could take them and walk out without paying, right?"

"So?"

"So now that you handed them to me, what's to stop me from doing that same thing when you walk away? You think because they were once locked up that prevents them from being stolen? I'll have to pay for them simply because they've been freed from vitamin prison?"

"That's why we have them locked up," he says, which immediately tells me two things. One is that he is not the brightest bulb in aisle five, and two, that this conversation has reached its natural conclusion.

I head home and walk Tara and Sonny, which has become the high point of every day. Nicole is having dinner with her parents; an event I avoided by saying I had to work. So after I walk and feed the dogs, I head down to Charlie's to watch some baseball and have dinner.

I figure I'll sit at the counter, but when I get here, I see Pete Stanton sitting at the same table he was at last time. The chair I sat in is empty; he appears to be alone.

"Hey, Pete, mind if I join you?" I ask, not because I want to but because it feels like I should.

"You bring your wallet?"

I reach back and pat my wallet. "Right here."

"Credit cards are in there?"

"Standing by and ready for action."

"Have a seat."

I sit down and order, and then I say, "Laurie is working out great. Thanks for the recommendation."

"That's because she is great."

"Some guy came to my office to threaten me, and she showed up and took care of him."

"You couldn't do it yourself?"

"Not even close."

He nods, reflecting his lack of surprise at the revelation. "Just stand behind her; you'll be fine."

We then spend a while eating, drinking beer, and watching the Mets game. They're down 3–0 in the fifth when the Mets score four runs, putting us both in a better mood.

"You ever heard of Jason Shore?" I ask.

"Of course. Why?"

"I think I've made an enemy out of him."

"Then don't let Laurie out of your sight."

"What do you know about him?"

"He's a scumbag. A wealthy one, which is the worst form of scumbag."

"Feel free to be more specific."

"He runs a loan-sharking operation for huge dollars, and once he has his hooks into you, he owns you. Or he owns your company. Usually both."

"Capable of murder?"

"If I had proof of it, he'd be having his fancy dinners in the prison mess hall. But I have no doubt."

"Stephen Pearson owed him big money."

Pete looks surprised. "Is that right, or is that your defense attorney bullshit?"

"I know it for a fact," I say, even though I don't. "With maybe a little bullshit thrown in."

He thinks for a moment. "Doesn't help you; the Pearson hit is not Shore's style."

"Why not?"

"Because there's too much evidence against your boy. Which either means the evidence is real, or it was set up to frame him. But that's not how Shore would do it. He wouldn't take the time or trouble to frame someone; there's be no reason to."

"Again . . . why not?"

"Because he'd use a pro to do it, and it would never come back to him. Framing someone else just means a trial and more scrutiny; there's no upside for Shore to do it that way."

"Maybe there's a reason we haven't figured out yet," I say.

"Possible, but doesn't matter."

"Why not?"

"Because maybe Shore had it done, or maybe he didn't. Either way you and Tierney are screwed."

On the way home from Charlie's I go out of my way to pass by the place where Ryan's car was ticketed the night of the explosion.

I'm not surprised to see that there are plenty of legal parking spaces; most people in this neighborhood keep their cars in their driveways or garages.

There is always the chance that something unusual was happening that night: maybe one of the neighbors was throwing a party or hosting a Springsteen concert. But there is also the chance that the car was parked illegally to strengthen the case against Ryan Tierney.

The car is a key piece of the prosecution's case. They have the motive in that Pearson had just fired Tierney. They have the means; Ryan literally had the explosive materials in his basement and the expertise to use them. The placement of the car gives him the opportunity; he seems to have been in a physical position to have accessed Pearson's car.

Nicole is home when I arrive, and she says she had a nice dinner with her parents. "Daddy still wants you to come work in his company; he asked if he should approach you again."

"What did you tell him?"

She smiles. "I didn't mention your ongoing root canal analogy; I just said this wasn't an ideal time."

"Good move." I grab the leashes to take the dogs on their

late walk, but Nicole says, "I took them already. We walked around the block a few times."

"You didn't have to do that."

"I actually liked it. They're so upbeat about everything. It's refreshing."

I nod. "Yes. They seem to have this life thing down pat."

"Let's go to bed, Andy."

"Works for me."

I'm awakened in the morning by a phone call from Sam; Nicole is sleeping next to me. "Andy, you coming into the office?" he asks.

"What time is it?"

"Let me look. . . . Six thirty. Is this too early?"

"It wouldn't be if I was a dairy farmer or a night watchman, Sam. But I'm a lawyer."

"Sorry. But I have the information on Pearson that you were looking for."

"Okay, I'll be down there as soon as I can."

I get up and take the dogs for their morning walk. I cut it a bit short, and I swear Tara looks at me in annoyance. "I'm sorry, Tara. I'll make it up to you guys tonight."

I wind up getting to the office at about eight thirty, and Sam is waiting for me with doughnuts, which almost makes the early wake-up worthwhile. He also has coffee, since he has one of those elusive coffee machines.

"Can I buy that machine from you?" I ask.

"Why don't you get your own?"

"Never mind. What did you find out?"

"Well, Stephen Pearson did not pay back those loans, if that's what they were, from his own personal account."

"Are you sure?"

Sam nods. "Positive. This was a rich guy, but not crazy rich. I mean, he wasn't going to starve or want for anything, but he also was not paying back two million dollars from his personal funds. There's no evidence of it at all."

"What about through another company? Any chance of that?"

"There's always a chance, but I don't see it anywhere. And there's certainly no connection between his personal account and another company. All of his income came from Pearson Trucking, plus dividends on some investments."

"So nothing unusual?"

"Depends on your definition. I'd be willing to bet he had a gambling problem."

"Why do you say that?" I ask, even though I know from Willie Tirico that it's true.

"He cashed a lot of checks. Not for the kind of money that pays off a two-million-dollar loan, but the kind that pays off bookmakers. He always took the cash near the end of a month."

"Interesting."

"Except on two occasions, he paid by check instead of cash. I don't know if he had neglected to get the cash or not, but it appears that those two times they relaxed their secrecy standards."

"When was this?"

"About eighteen months ago, and four months after that. He wrote the check to a Robert Dent. Dent has been arrested four times for illegal bookmaking, but each time the charges were dropped or reduced to a misdemeanor."

I don't want to ask the question, but I have to. "You accessed his arrest records?"

"I did. They're not particularly secure."

"Is there anything you can't access?"

Sam shrugs. "Maybe the nuclear codes?"

"So how much in total did he pay to Dent?"

"Well, I didn't add it up, but it's approximately ten thousand a month for two years, so almost a quarter mil. That's assuming the cash all went to Dent as well."

"Dent never paid him? So he never won?"

"Doesn't seem like it."

I nod. "Maybe he kept betting on the Mets and Giants. Is there anything else?"

Sam nods. "One more thing. Pearson kept an apartment in the Hudson Towers in Fort Lee. He often rented it out, but had owned it for three years."

"I wonder why. The guy lived in Englewood Cliffs, which is close by. Why would he need a second place to stay? Unless he wasn't alone when he was staying there."

"I can't help you with that."

I hear the phone ringing in my office, so I head down there to answer it.

It's Laurie. "Anna Pearson finally called me back. She's willing to meet with you this morning."

"Excellent." I then tell Laurie about Pearson's apparent gambling losses and ask her to check out Robert Dent just in case, which she says she will do right away.

I don't think Dent is a likely candidate for the role of murderer in this play. Pearson was paying him regularly; there's no reason to kill a guy when he's a reliable supply of money. The opposite would be true. But it can't hurt to look into it and see if there's anything there.

"Two other things." I tell Laurie about the apartment that Pearson had in Hudson Towers. "See if you can find out how often he stayed there, and whether he was alone. I have information that fidelity was not his strong point."

"I'll get right on it."

While Laurie is doing all that, I will go meet with the widow Pearson.

S am said that Stephen Pearson was not uber-wealthy, but you would never know that by his house.

It is one of the nicest houses in Englewood Cliffs, which means it's one of the nicest houses, period. There's a Mercedes at the end of the long driveway leading to the house, and when I get out of the car, I see a pool and tennis court in the back.

Just based on the trappings, I don't think I'm going to need to hold a benefit dinner for Anna Pearson.

I expect a butler to greet me at the door, but I get Anna herself. She's dressed casually in jeans and a short jacket and has a pair of sunglasses in her hair above her forehead. Since there's a roof on the house, I'm not sure why she's worried about glare.

"Mr. Carpenter, you're prompt. Good. That's a lawyer thing."

"I wasn't aware of that. But I try not to keep people waiting."

"Come in. Would you like to sit in the den or out by the pool?"

"Den works well. Love of air-conditioning is another lawyer thing."

"Fine. Coffee?"

"If you're having some."

She points to a room off the foyer and suggests I wait in there. It's a den, with a fireplace so large that it would take a chopped-up giant sequoia to fill it up.

As I wait, I notice that there are at least seven photos of her and Stephen Pearson. They all make them look like a happy, doting couple.

She comes in with the coffee and sets it down. "Were you surprised that I agreed to talk with you?"

"To a degree, yes. Many people in your position would consider me the enemy."

"Are you?"

"Not now. Maybe later. Right now I'm just trying to find out the truth about who killed your husband. So at least for the moment I see us as allies."

"But if the guilty party turns out to be your client, you will still work to set him free?"

I nod. "It's my job. But I don't think it will come to that."

"Because Ryan is wrongly accused?"

"I'm starting to believe that, yes."

"On the one hand I hope that's true, because I always liked Ryan. But on the other hand, I would then fear that the real killer would never be held to account."

She puts down her coffee cup. "So, what would you like to ask me?"

"How much do you know about the inner workings of Pearson Trucking?"

"Not very much, I'm afraid, though that will be changing soon."

"You intend to become active?"

"I intend to become knowledgeable. That will be a first step that will let me decide where to go from there."

"Does the name Jason Shore mean anything to you?"

"No. Should it?"

"He's an investor in Pearson Trucking."

"Then I will get to know him."

"So tell me about Stephen's enemies."

"He didn't have any to speak of," she says quickly.

"He had at least one."

She frowns. "I'll grant you that. But I have no knowledge of it."

"Did he seem particularly stressed or concerned about anything in the days and weeks before his death?"

"Not that I noticed. But Stephen had the capacity to keep things concealed."

"Maybe his gambling was not going well and was causing pressure?"

She smiles. "You do your homework."

I return the smile. "It's a lawyer thing."

"I am not aware of any such gambling concerns; Stephen did not risk amounts that were important to our lifestyle."

"So things were fine between you?"

"Are you trying to ask me tactfully about Stephen's infidelities?"

"What gave it away?"

"We had what I would not call an open marriage, but it was not a restrictive one either. Stephen knew the limits and stayed within them. Technically I could have done the same had I wanted to."

"Can you give me any names of people that were within his limits?"

"I cannot. He did not share that information with me, though I suppose he would have if I requested it. But I can assure you that he was not involved with anyone who would blow up his car. He had much better taste and instincts than that."

"How well do you know Ryan Tierney? You said you liked him."

"Very well. Ryan and Willie Tirico and Stephen go way back."

"When you heard that Ryan was arrested, what was your first reaction?"

"Disbelief; I did not think it possible that he would have done this."

"And now?"

"Continued disbelief."

Nicole, there is something you should know," I say, while we are sitting in the den after dinner.

"I don't like conversations that start with a sentence like that."

I nod. "Sorry, I don't either. So I'll get right to the point. I've been threatened."

Her face shows obvious surprise at what I said; I think she was expecting something personal about our relationship. "Threatened? What does that mean? Who threatened you?"

"His name is Victor Cobb. He broke into my office and warned me about my actions on the case, that I was worrying people about what I might find out."

"What did you do?"

"Laurie Collins showed up and had him arrested."

"So where is he now?"

"Either in jail or out on bail. But he doesn't matter; it's the people that sent him that are the danger."

"Who are they?"

"I don't know for sure." That's technically true, though I obviously believe it was Jason Shore. I don't want to share that with Nicole for various reasons, and I also don't think it's helpful to her to know that.

Nicole stands up and starts to pace around the room,

talking as she does. "Are you still doing what they warned you about?"

"I am. Or at least I'm trying to. They must think I know more than I do."

"When did this happen?"

"A few days ago."

"And you waited until now to tell me?"

"I did."

"Why did you tell me at all?"

"I thought you had a right to know. You're my wife; you're involved."

"Is it because they could come here? If they could break into your office, they could break into our home?"

"It's possible, but very unlikely."

"So killers possibly could come into our home, but we doubt it will happen? That's supposed to make me feel secure?"

"My goal in telling you was not to make you feel secure; I wish that I could. It was to make you aware of what is going on."

"Andy, it is not fair that I have to be a part of this world. Of threats, of explosions, of murders. It is not something I signed up for. 'Till death do us part' was not meant to be imminent."

"It's my job, Nicole."

"It doesn't have to be. You can have a job where you make ten times the money and the biggest danger is that you'll have too many martinis at lunch. What is so terrible about that?"

"It is not what I want to do. It is not how I want to spend my life."

"Are you ever going to get this out of your system?"

"It's not a virus, Nicole."

"That's a matter of opinion, Andy. Good night."

She turns and goes upstairs to our bedroom, leaving me with my wine, Tara, and Sonny. I can't blame her; it's totally unfair that I put her in this situation. And she is right: she did not sign up for this.

Tara comes over and puts her head on my knee.

"Well, Tara, that went well."

My name is Andy Carpenter. I'm an attorney representing a client in a case that Mr. Shore has an interest in."

I'm taking a shot and calling Jason Shore. I don't know who I'm talking to, but it's most likely an assistant who answers his phone and screens his calls.

"Hold on," the person says, rather gruffly. It doesn't sound like Shore sends his assistants to charm school.

It's almost five minutes until the guy comes back. "What do you want?"

"To meet with Shore; I have some questions for him."

"Email me your questions. If he wants to answer them, he will."

This guy is annoying me. "Actually, that's not how this is going to work. He can meet with me and we can have a nice conversation, or he can answer the questions under oath, either in a deposition or a courtroom per a lawful subpoena. Emails will not be involved."

"I will call you back. Or I won't."

He hangs up the phone; I don't think I intimidated him.

Thirty seconds later the phone rings again, leading me to believe that maybe I've underestimated my impact. That's until I see on the caller ID that it's Laurie.

"Andy, I'm at Hudson Towers. I'm going to talk to one of the doormen. You might want to sit in on it."

"Okay, I'll come down there. I'm at the office, so—"

She interrupts, "No, he's not here. I'll pick you up in a few."

I have no idea why the Hudson Towers doorman is not at Hudson Towers, but I find out as soon as she picks me up. "I spoke to the day guy," she says. "We're going to talk to the night guy. He's waiting for us at his apartment."

It turns out his name is Roger Champlin, and he lives in a garden apartment in Lodi. He's waiting for us in front when we pull up. I'm not sure why; maybe it's doorman practice.

He greets us with a smile and we go inside. He introduces us to his wife, who has a similar welcoming smile, but we decline her offer of something to eat or drink. I should say that Laurie quickly declines, which leaves me too uncomfortable to ask what the options are.

We sit in what is either their den or living room and Laurie starts. "I know Mr. Walling told you we want to talk about Stephen Pearson." Then she turns to me and says, "Mr. Walling is the doorman at the Hudson Towers building during the day."

"Right," Champlin says. "I'm there five nights a week; I'm off Monday and Tuesday. Terrible about what happened to Mr. Pearson."

"Yes, it is," Laurie says.

"I'm not sure I should be talking about him like this," Champlin says. "As you can imagine, sometimes people rely on us to be discreet."

"I know. But in this case, he would be relying on you to help in the effort to find his killer."

"I guess so," Champlin says, still unsure. "What is it you want to know?"

"How often did Mr. Pearson use the apartment?"

"Maybe two or three times a week. That's not counting the times he might have used it when I wasn't there."

"Understood," Laurie says. "Was he usually alone, or with someone?"

"With someone. There were times he was alone, but they were rare. Maybe ten percent of the time."

"And it was with a woman?" she asks.

"Yes."

"Always the same one?"

"No, definitely not. He went through them fairly quickly." Then Champlin seems to realize he may have said something inappropriate or insensitive, so he adds, "Sorry."

"That's fine," Laurie says in a reassuring voice. She's good at this. "But sometimes the same woman was with him a number of times?"

"Yes. In a typical period of, say, six weeks, there might be two or three women that were there a bunch of times. Maybe one of them would be with him on a Wednesday and again on Sunday. But there might be a different woman on Friday."

"Do you know any of their names?"

"No, he never introduced me."

"Would you recognize them if you saw them?"

"Some of them, I think so. Sure."

"Mr. Walling said that when Mr. Pearson would leave in the morning, he was always alone."

Champlin nods. "Right. The women always left very early in the morning, while I was still on."

"And Mr. Pearson did not leave with them?"

"Right. He did not."

I haven't said two words the entire time we've been here; Laurie has covered it quite well. We both thank him for his time and then leave.

When we get in the car, Laurie says, "Pearson certainly got around."

"Yes. But it's hard to see how it got him killed."

"Maybe his wife got fed up and hired someone? She wound up with the business, the house, and all the money."

"Possible. She claimed she knew all about what he was doing and was fine with it. And—"

I'm interrupted by the ringing of my cell phone. The caller ID says PRIVATE CALL.

"Hello."

"Mr. Shore will see you at his office tomorrow at two P.M."

"Good. That will give me time to get a mani-pedi."

Daddy, as you know, has a private security firm on retainer. As a senator and businessman, he needs it," Nicole says during dinner.

"I know," I say. "They're always with him when he's out."

She nods. "And they are protecting his home when he and Rita are home." Nicole fortunately refers to her stepmother as Rita, and not Stepmommy.

"Right." I know where this is going.

"He's offered to provide you the same service until the end of this case you're working on."

"Very generous of him."

"I think so too."

"I'm willing to compromise on this. They can watch over you and watch over the house while you're at home. But I cannot have people following me while I do my job. It just doesn't work for me."

"I'm sorry, Andy. But I'm not being clear. I'm not going to be here. I can't live with this hanging over my head, over our heads. This is about you. Daddy will provide the protection for you. I will be somewhere safe."

I was wrong; I did not know where this was going. "You're leaving again?"

"You've set up a situation where I have no choice. I don't

even feel like I am leaving voluntarily; I feel like you're throwing me out."

"I am not throwing you out. I want you to stay. Your father can protect you; which gives you nothing to worry about."

"I'll worry about you, Andy. I love you. But I can't let you introduce me to the world you've chosen to live in."

"I'm a lawyer, Nicole. My career world is the courtroom. The threat I received was an unusual occurrence; my job is not one of personal danger. I'm not driving a Humvee in Afghanistan."

"I'm not trying to convince you anymore, Andy. I am aware that the ship has sailed."

"So you're saying that you're leaving permanently?" I understand her position, but it's becoming frustrating and annoying. Our marriage has become a revolving door.

"No, I need to do a lot of thinking. But I certainly won't be back before the end of your case. Which, by the way, I hope you win . . . if that means justice prevails."

"When are you leaving?"

"When we finish dinner."

"I'll take care of the dishes."

should go with you," Laurie said when she heard I was going to meet with Shore.

"Why? You think he's going to shoot me in his office?"

"Of course not. I think he'll have his people take you out into the woods and shoot you there."

"Then I'll be one with nature. But I think the conversation will go better if I go it alone."

"What is it you're trying to accomplish?"

"Nothing concrete. I'm just trying to shake things up and apply pressure. People under pressure tend to make mistakes. The status quo is not working for us."

"Where is his office?"

I tell her the address and the time of the meeting. "I'll be nearby," she says. "Put my phone number on your phone so you just have to press a button."

"I don't think you respect my toughness and courage."

"Guilty as charged."

"Thanks."

On the way to Shore's office in Englewood, I'm thinking maybe I should have let Laurie come along. I have no idea if Shore was involved with the car bombing, but Pete Stanton clearly said he considered Shore quite capable of murder.

Logic says I am in no danger, at least during this meeting.

Shore would certainly be aware of the possibility that I have told people where I'm going; if I didn't return, he would be the natural suspect.

More likely, sometime in the days after this meeting, he could easily have someone put a bullet in my head.

There, now I feel much better.

Shore's company has a three-story, modern-looking building on Grand Avenue. I park the car down the street and walk toward it, and when I get there, I see a police car parked in front.

A male cop is in the driver's seat and Laurie Collins is his passenger. She waves to me and smiles as I pass by; when she said she'd be close by, she wasn't kidding. And she also found a way to send a message to Jason Shore, just in case.

I enter the lobby and tell the receptionist at the desk that Andy Carpenter is here to see Jason Shore. She seems pleasant enough; she probably isn't one of the enforcers or leg breakers that Shore is said to employ. That's a shame because, since she's maybe five foot two and 110 pounds, I could probably hold my own with her.

About five minutes later, a man who I recognize as Kenneth Burks gets off the elevator. He's the guy who has been going to see Mike Shaffer at his office, and very probably the one who used to meet with Stephen Pearson. He's a lot bigger than the photo made him seem.

"Follow me," he says, dispensing with the pleasantries. Before he turns, he looks through the glass door and sees the police car. He then looks at me, apparently registering that the car and I are connected. He frowns and walks toward the elevator, and I follow.

The ride up two floors takes about fifteen seconds, but it feels like a month. Neither of us says a word, and when the door opens, he walks out. I'm sure he expects me to follow him, but I'm also sure he'd be fine if I didn't.

I follow him down the hall, reminding myself that I need to act confident and in control, even though I am neither confident nor in control.

He leads me into an office, where a man I assume to be Jason Shore is sitting at his desk. He doesn't bother to get up and makes no effort to shake hands. "Andy Carpenter," he says.

"Really? That's my name also. Talk about a small world."

"Sit down," he says.

I point to Burks. "Not until he's out of here."

"He works for me," Shore says.

"Then you can read him the minutes of our meeting after I leave." I have no reason to not want Burks here, other than to show that I can dictate the terms.

Shore looks at Burks, and I swear Shore does not so much as move a facial muscle. Yet there must be some unspoken communication because Burks silently gets up and leaves the room, closing the door behind him.

"How did you do that?" I ask.

"Is that the question you came to ask me?"

"No. I came to ask you about your investment in Pearson Trucking."

"What makes you think I have such an investment?"

I probably shouldn't tell him that Sam Willis hacked into their financials, and I have already decided on a different approach. "Not *what* makes me think it. It's *who* makes me think it, and the answer is Mike Shaffer."

I have no concern about throwing Shaffer under the bus. If everything is on the up-and-up, then Shaffer as controller has the right to tell me anything he wants. If Shaffer is instead in some kind of illegal conspiracy with Shore, possibly including murder, then let the two bad guys fight it out.

"Is that right?" he asks.

"It's right to the tune of more than two million dollars. So here's my first question. How is it you lent them two million dollars, they turned around the company, and they haven't paid you back a dime?"

"I don't discuss my business dealings with nobody lawyers."

"Or maybe you showed your displeasure with not being paid back by, oh, I don't know . . . I'm just spitballing here . . . blowing up a car."

"If that's your defense, your client is going away for a long time."

"Maybe, but not before we drag you through the mud in open court."

"I believe this meeting is over."

"It's been a real treat." I turn and leave. Once I'm outside the door, I see Burks standing there, staring at me.

"Mr. Shore will see you now," I say.

I go down the elevator and leave. The police car, Laurie in the passenger seat, is still there. I wave, and she smiles as they pull away.

know I shouldn't call Sam with another request for illegal hacking, but I can't help it.

"Sam, I need you to find out whatever you can about Jason Shore's finances."

"I'm on it."

"Is there a chance you can do so legally?" I already know the answer. I am asking Sam to criminally trespass, as surely as if I were sneaking Sam into Shore's office and telling Sam to rummage through the filing cabinets.

"Zero. But don't worry, Andy. It's not going to bite us in the ass."

"Famous last words."

"Trust me, Andy. Now what do you want to know about Jason Shore and his money?"

"I have no idea."

"That should be easy to find."

I head home to what is once again an empty house, at least as far as humans are concerned. Tara and Sonny are here to greet me at the door. It's incredibly comforting; they are here for me no matter how many mass murderers I might defend, and no matter how many times I am threatened by thugs and killers.

All I definitely accomplished by meeting with Shore was to create enemies. Certainly Shore and Kenneth Burks will not be inviting me to brunch at their club anytime soon, and Mike Shaffer will soon be sticking pins in an Andy Carpenter voodoo doll.

I'd like to be a fly on the wall in the next conversation that either Shore or Burks has with Shaffer. I lied and told them that Shaffer revealed their involvement in Pearson Trucking to me. I'm sure they believed me, since they are unaware of any other way I could have found out.

Shaffer's apparent secrecy breach will undoubtedly land him in deep trouble with them. I can't say I am concerned for him. I told the lie mostly to shake things up and to create discord within the group I view as the conspirators.

If that discord becomes great enough that Shaffer starts to worry about starting his car in the morning, maybe he'll flip on them and reveal what is going on. The chances are that he is just a follower in this whole thing; Pearson must have been the initial driving force.

But it still makes no sense to me that they would have killed Pearson in the way they did, simply for nonpayment of his debt. They would have other, interim steps to encourage payment, but they don't seem to have employed them. So maybe Shaffer is a key guy, and Pearson was just in the way.

One of the things I hope Sam uncovers is whether this is part of a pattern. If Shore has behaved the same way with other companies, it gives me more chances to uncover the reason.

Unfortunately, hovering over all this is that if I knew for certain that Shore had Pearson and the others killed, right now there is nothing I can do with it. There is no evidence implicating him and plenty implicating Ryan Tierney.

The simple fact is that the reason there is so much evidence against Ryan is because Ryan could be guilty. If you were betting on it, that would be the way to bet.

Two things could simultaneously be true. Jason Shore could have been pressuring Pearson to repay the debt, or could have had some other conspiracy going on with him, but Ryan could still have set off the bomb.

It's all frustrating and it's entirely possible that it's turning me into a bit of a nutcase. For instance, I'm starting to find myself talking to Tara and Sonny when we go on our walks.

We have a small park not far from our house and I've been walking them through there. They seem to love it, and there usually aren't any people around to hear me talking to the dogs about the case.

"Tara, I don't see what Shore was getting from the relationship with Pearson, and I certainly don't see why he would kill him before getting paid back. Do you?"

Not a word from Tara, nor Sonny, for that matter. They either can't figure it out either or want me to come to it on my own.

"It doesn't seem as if Pearson gave Shore an equity position in the company, even though Laurie said that's how he operates with loans that are not repaid.

"We're going on two years; he would have wanted to take some money out by now or fully take over the company."

The dogs obviously have nothing to say, so we finish the walk and head home. Nicole has only been gone one day, but her absence is obvious from just looking around the house.

For one thing, there are dirty dishes in the sink. For another, the bed isn't made. Making a bed never made sense to me since it is inevitably going to be unmade at the end of the day.

Nicole was rigid about bed-making, but she did the work; she did not expect me to do it. For a woman who grew up with a maid and a butler, she has a remarkably strong work ethic.

She has something on the bed, or under it, called a dust ruffle. She's mentioned it a few times, but I have no idea what it is, or what might be the purpose of it.

Does it catch dust in some kind of ruffle? What the hell is a ruffle? And if it catches the dust, do I need to empty it at some point? Even vacuum cleaner bags eventually have to be emptied or replaced. Do I need to get a backup ruffle? Is there a ruffle store near here? I'll need to find all this out if Nicole's absence lasts.

I can't worry about it now. I go through discovery papers with Tara's head in my lap. Just before I stop, I ask her, "What could Pearson have had that helped him keep Shore off his back?"

But before Tara can answer, it comes to me.

Trucks.

And the things they could carry.

W hy the hell are you lying about me?"

That's how Mike Shaffer starts our conversation when I answer my phone. He doesn't sound happy, which does not come as a surprise; I have trouble making friends.

I cover the phone and mouth to Laurie that it's Shaffer calling. "And he's pissed," I whisper.

"I don't know what you mean," I say to Shaffer.

"You damn well do. You told Jason Shore that I revealed his investment to you. That's bullshit and you know it."

"It happens to be true; you did tell me about Shore. I just had the timing wrong."

"What the hell are you talking about?"

"You know about my conversation with Shore. Which means he called you to complain about telling me about the money he pumped into the company. Which confirms that I was right about him being the pump-er and your company being the pump-ee. So you did tell me, you just waited until now to do it."

"You don't know what you are getting into, Carpenter. And you sure as hell don't know who you are messing with."

"And you better jump ship and tell what you know before it's too late, Shaffer. Because every time I learn something, and I plan on learning plenty, I'm going to tell Shore I got it from you."

"You were warned." He hangs up.

"Always a pleasure," I say to the dead phone.

Laurie is at the house for our morning meeting. We've decided to meet briefly each day to inform each other about anything we've learned. I describe the Shaffer conversation to her.

"You obviously hit a nerve with Shore," she says.

"That was the plan. But it's a long way from doing us any good. At least now we know for certain that Shore is deeply involved with Pearson Trucking. Before this I only assumed so because Kenneth Burks was visiting Stephen Pearson and then Mike Shaffer."

"I know I've said this before, but you could be in some danger here."

"I don't think so. If they went after me, it would only draw much more attention to the situation. I doubt that they want that."

"So what's your biggest worry?"

"That we're operating on separate tracks and that they never cross. We think Shore might have something illegal going on with Pearson Trucking, or at least he's putting intense pressure on them. And we might find out what's going on there, or we might not. But the other track is the bombing, and that might not have anything to do with Jason Shore at all."

"So all we can do is follow both tracks and see where they lead."

"Exactly."

"You have anything for me to do?"

"Yes. When they got the investment, Pearson Trucking refrigerated a bunch of their trucks and bought some more. Then they hired drivers for them. I want to know how those drivers were hired . . . where they came from."

"Okay. Why the interest?"

"Because if Pearson is not paying back the loan, and if Shore isn't taking over the company, then the only thing Pearson could have to offer them are the trucks. I don't know how Shore could be using them, but it's worth pursuing."

"Sounds logical."

"Maybe you could put the other guy, Marcus Clark, on it also."

"He's not available right now," she says. Then, "Meet here again tomorrow morning?"

"Yes. I hate leaving the dogs alone all day."

"Nicole is out of town?"

"We're separated . . . I think."

"Oh . . . I'm sorry to hear that. . . . You 'think'?"

I laugh. "I didn't mean it that way. I know we're separated, just not sure for how long or if it's permanent. Nicole is somewhat unhappy with my career path and the danger it represents."

Laurie nods. "I can see that. It can be scary for people who aren't part of this world."

"Are you married?" The words came out without my meaning them to. I wanted to be more subtle, but subtlety has never been part of my skill set.

"No."

I should not be glad about that and I should not be thinking about Laurie the way I am. But since introspection is even lower on my list of talents than subtlety, I'm not going to focus on that now.

"Okay, let's get to work," I say.

S am tells me he has a report on Jason Shore's business
operation to give me.

He offers to come to the house, but I tell him that I'll meet
him at the office. I don't want to take Sam away from his computer, and he also has an accountant business to run when he's
not playing detective for me.

I also have a couple of stops I want to make. The first is
in Lodi, where Ryan Tierney's house has stood empty since
his arrest. I've cleared it with Karen Vincent to go inside, although it wasn't necessary, since the police have long finished
their forensic work there.

Tierney's car is still in his driveway, and it's parked less
than ten feet from the side of the house. It's obviously daylight, but I don't see any outside lights that would cover this
area. The car is locked. I don't know if Ryan always locked
it when it's parked here, but if he does, it makes it even less
likely that someone stole it, drove it away, and then returned
it that night, all without it being noticed.

I go inside and start out in the basement. This is clearly
where Ryan created his fireworks; he has openly admitted it.
There are three tables set up, with the supplies in boxes along
the walls. I wonder if it's safe just sitting here like this; in any
event I'm not going to stay long.

I walk around the house, mainly to see where various rooms

are in relation to the driveway. The kitchen is on the first floor, on that side of the house. It's doubtful that Ryan was hanging out in the kitchen at that hour since it was well past dinnertime.

The den, which houses a large-screen TV, is on that side of the house, opposite the driveway. Upstairs, the bedroom is also on that side of the house. If Ryan was in the den or bedroom, it's credible that he may not have heard the car being driven away, but it will be a hard sell to the jury.

Before going back to the office, I stop off at Gilmore's Gym in Garfield. I want to talk to Randy Clemons again about his wife, Denise, Pearson's assistant who was also killed in the explosion. I didn't call ahead since we didn't part as best buddies the last time we spoke.

This is the same time of day I met him here last time, and Clemons struck me as the type who is religious about his workouts. If he's not here, then no harm, no foul.

But he is here, slaving and sweating away on another machine that I could never figure out how to work, and I have no interest in trying. But Clemons has no problem with it; this guy looks like he could bench-press Peru.

He's turned away from me, and the only reason I know it's him, and not some other behemoth, is the prosthetic leg.

I stand there for three or four minutes; my self-preservation instinct tells me that this is not a guy who likes his workouts interrupted. He finally finishes, grabs his towel, and walks toward me. He's either going to the locker room or the small café where he had his disgustingly healthy smoothie the last time.

He's almost upon me when he actually sees me. He does not light up with delighted recognition; he merely says, "You're back."

"I was hoping to buy you a smoothie."

He nods. "Good enough."

We walk into the café. Clemons sits at a table and calls to the man behind the counter. "My regular, Tommy, and he's buying."

Tommy springs into action and I walk over and pay, after which I bring the smoothie back to Clemons. I take the seat opposite him as he drinks it.

"I asked around about you down at the precinct," he says. "I didn't know you were Nelson Carpenter's son."

"I should carry a sign."

"He pissed at you for going to the other side?"

"It doesn't fulfill a life's dream for him."

Clemons laughs. "I can imagine." Then, "How's your case going?"

"It's a marathon, not a sprint."

"You a runner?"

"Only if I'm being chased."

"So let me guess: you have more questions for me. I have nothing that can help you, and I wouldn't if I could. I want your boy in prison."

"I'll take a shot anyway. You ever heard of Jason Shore?"

He pauses to think for maybe thirty seconds. "I think so. I think Denise might have mentioned him."

"In what context?"

"I don't remember; must have had something to do with the company."

"Was she worried about him?"

He shakes his head. "I doubt it. I'd remember something like that; I was protective of Denise . . . though not protective enough, as it turned out."

"You couldn't have known what was going to happen."

"That's what I tell myself."

"What did Denise think of Stephen Pearson?"

"She liked him. He was respectful of her, paid her well."

"Did she ever mention that he was unfaithful to his wife?"

Clemons frowns. "What does that have to do with any-thing?"

"I just ask questions. Sometimes the answers matter, some-times they don't. I never know until I know."

"Yeah. She knew about what he was doing. But she never covered for him."

"Did she ever mention the names of the women?"

"Not to me."

"Did she ever talk about how Pearson's wife felt about it?"

"Not to me."

"You're not being at all helpful."

He smiles. "Mission accomplished."

J ason Shore's finances are extremely complicated, as
are his businesses," Sam says.

"In fact, it's hard to separate the two. And it's especially difficult because all his businesses are privately owned."

"I understand, just tell me what you know."

"Shore's main company is called JM Distribution, which makes it no surprise that he is a distributor."

"What does he distribute?"

"He doesn't really seem to have a specialty; toys, small kitchen appliances, flatware, televisions, and quite a bit more. A lot of it is in plastic. But one of the largest single items is food."

"That would explain the refrigerated trucks," I say. "Where does he get the stuff he distributes?"

"Various places; he has contracts in place with some manu-facturers. He imports a great deal of it."

"Does he own a piece of the manufacturers he deals with?"

"I really haven't looked at that. It's possible he loaned them money in the same way he did with Pearson, but I just don't know."

"How much money does he make through his distribution company? What are we talking about?"

"Not as much as you think, at least regarding what's out in the open, or at least open enough for me to get to it. Shore's personal accounts are way too healthy for this company to be his main source of income. He also has offshore accounts that I can't access; no one can."

"So Pearson's trucks are part of his distribution network?"

"I can only assume that," Sam says.

"Has he paid for the use of those trucks?"

Sam shakes his head. "Nothing beyond the two million plus he had put in. But that amount of money is way disproportionate, and he would have been crazy to pay so much of it up front."

"Shore is many things, but he's not crazy. Does he have a main center of operations?"

Sam nods and takes a piece of paper out of his pocket, unfolding it as he does. "He has an enormous warehouse in Parsippany. I found it on Google Maps; here's an overhead shot. It's like the size of three football fields."

"So that's the business end. What about Shore's personal accounts?"

"Very hard to tell because, like I said, much of it is hidden offshore in inaccessible accounts. But the guy is loaded; that much is clear. I suspect that those accounts are where the money he loans out comes from, and where repayments would go."

"But Pearson never made any repayments? You're sure of that?" As I'm asking the question, I realize I am addicted to Sam's getting information through illegal hacking. It's going to be hard to quit.

"As sure as I can be. But remember, I can't tell that from the Shore side; so much of what he does is hidden. I don't see any payments from the Pearson side."

I thank Sam and head home. I'm missing Nicole, but I know from the last time she left that it's a feeling that comes and goes. I still love her, but I don't love the arguing or the guilt I feel for upending her life.

There is much to be said for being alone, as well, but right now I am wishing that she were here.

But what we have at this point is not a real marriage. I know that we are going to have to either fully commit, or not. I also know that it can't take place until after this case is concluded.

Maybe I should go to work for her father's company. I'll make a fortune, not have to deal with criminals, and have a comfortable life.

Most important, I will never have to fail to prevent an innocent person from going to prison, and I will never succeed in helping a guilty person get away with the crime he committed.

With the trial bearing down on me, I'm not sure why I don't become Andy Carpenter, the wealthy, married, big-time corporate lawyer.

On the way home I stop and pick up a frozen pizza, because for the moment I am Andy Carpenter, the struggling, separated, legal nobody.

It feels nice to be met at the door by Tara and Sonny.

They seem genuinely thrilled to see me, and the feeling is mutual. I don't know how anything is going to play out in my personal or business life, but no matter what, getting them is always going to be a great decision.

I'm really hungry and I know they are as well, so I take them for a quick walk and promise them we'll take a longer one later. For now we go home and I feed them and bake the frozen pizza for myself.

It says to preheat the oven, but I've never had the patience for that, so I just shove it in. That works just fine.

I turn on the Mets game and watch a few innings. I'm tired and want to go to sleep, but I don't want to walk the dogs too early, since they'll have to be inside all night. I can get up at three in the morning and go to the bathroom, they can't.

It's around nine thirty when I finally take them. We walk the two blocks and enter the park. It's pretty dark in here, but we can see just well enough to walk in the moonlight without banging into trees.

I don't feel unsafe; Franklin Lakes is not the kind of town you worry in. I know that violence and crime can happen anywhere, but somehow there is a secure vibe here.

Unfortunately, safety is not all that I'm looking for. Franklin Lakes just does not feel like home; Paterson feels like home. Maybe if Nicole doesn't come back, I'll move there. But like in everything else these days, for now I don't have enough information to make informed decisions.

We're walking in the park when suddenly I hear an angry growl. For a moment I don't know where it's coming from, but then I hear it again and I realize it's Tara making the noise. She and Sonny have stopped in their tracks; something has upset and angered Tara, exposing a side of her I've not seen before.

I'm thinking it must be an animal she's discovered, and that worries me. There have been reports of coyotes in the area, and warnings have been issued that people should take care to protect their small dogs. Tara is not a small dog, but I still worry for her, and I worry for Sonny even more.

"Hold it right there, lawyer."

It's a voice from up ahead in the darkness, and I'm willing to bet that it's not a coyote speaking. Suddenly a new sound is introduced, and I realize it's my heart pounding; it's as if I have been dropped into an adrenaline bath.

Even in my panicked state, I realize that this is not a robbery. The voice called me "lawyer," which means they know who I am, which means they've been waiting for me. Which makes this far scarier because I cannot save myself by surrendering my wallet.

I think I can make out two shapes in the distance, and they seem to be moving toward me. I can see a glint of light off something in one of their hands, and I'm betting it's not a subpoena.

So I start to run in the opposite direction. I'm still holding on to the leashes; I'm not sure why. The dogs would be better off being as far away from me as possible.

I can hear movement behind me, and I know the assailants

are chasing me. It will not be easy to shoot accurately in the darkness, so I'm sure they want to be as close as possible before firing their deadly shots, if that's what they're going to do.

I trip and fall, maybe over one of the leashes, I'm not sure. The shapes are getting close to me . . . they are less than twenty yards away. They are going to kill me and there is nothing I can do about it.

"People know where I am," I say.

"Good. Then they can find your body."

"Don't do this."

"You were warned. Say good-bye, lawyer."

I cringe and a shot rings out. But I'm not hit, and while the dogs have reacted to the shot, they don't seem to be hit either. There is some movement, and I hear something between a scream and a grunt.

Then everything is still. I peer ahead and don't see the two shapes anymore. At first I don't know what to do. I know what I should do: I should run away, I need to get the hell out of here.

But I can't; I need to find out what happened. So I cautiously approach where the two shapes were. And then I see them, lying on the ground. I can't see if they've been shot, or if they're alive or dead, and I'm not waiting to find out.

I turn around and run out of the park. Tara and Sonny are delighted by the sudden burst of energy, and they pull me along on their leashes. We run all the way home, by which point I am gasping for breath.

Once I'm able to speak, I call 911 and tell them where I am, and that there are two bodies in the park, maybe dead . . . I don't know for sure. I claim that I saw them while I was walking my dogs. It's true, but leaves out a key detail, like they were there to kill me.

The 911 operator tells me to stay where I am, that the police will come to me. She is certainly right about that; three squad cars are here within five minutes.

I recount what happened, or at least my current version of what happened, and we're off to the park, with me in the backseat of one of the cars. On the way I reflect on my instinct to withhold the full truth.

Somebody saved my life tonight, someone who didn't appear after he or she did so. I owe that person as much as I have ever owed anyone, and if they want to retreat into the darkness, I am not going to give the police a reason to shine a light on them.

If they were there to protect me, then they have a connection to me, a connection that the police could uncover if they have reason to believe that I was the target.

I don't know who it was, but I can only think of three possibilities. One is Laurie, though I doubt that. As an ex-cop, I would think she would have felt an obligation to reveal herself. She did nothing wrong; she was saving my life.

Two is Marcus Clark. Laurie said that he was unavailable to look into the situation at Pearson Trucking. It's possible that unavailability was caused by his protecting me on her instructions.

The third is that I am not Jason Shore's only enemy. Maybe someone else wants to take him down as well, and they believe that I represent their best chance to do that. They, whoever they are, would therefore want to keep me alive.

We arrive at the park and I lead the officers toward where the two bodies are. I have this sudden fear that they will not be there anymore, though I'm not sure that would be a bad thing for me.

But they are there, and as soon as the cops see them, they

move me back from the immediate area and spring into action. Within what seems like seconds, at least six other squad cars show up, and the area is bathed in floodlights.

The cops move me even farther back and ask me to sit in the back of one of their cars. I can see them spreading out, guns drawn, searching the area for possible continued dangers.

Five minutes later I get a text from Laurie that simply asks, "Can you talk?"

I respond with "Not now . . . I'm with the police. I accidentally happened upon two bodies in the park." If she knows what went on tonight, and I suspect from her "Can you talk?" message that she does, then my response tells her the position I am taking.

"Call me when you can," she texts.

I would love nothing more than to get out of here and go home, but that is going to take a while.

"Come with me, Andy," says Pete Stanton.

Pete and I walk through the park, far enough away from the crowd that no one can hear us.

He tells me that a Franklin Lakes cop who he knows had called him with a heads-up as to what was going on. Pete asks me to tell him everything that happened, then just listens as I give the short response.

"I was walking the dogs and Tara reacted strangely to something. I walked over to see what it was; I figured it would be a dead animal or something. I saw the two bodies and ran the hell back to the house."

"So you don't know who those guys are?"

"No idea."

"Or what they were doing here?"

"No."

"Or who killed them?"

"Nope. So they're both dead?"

"Yeah. One was shot; one was smashed in the head."

"With a club or something?"

"Or a really powerful fist or elbow. The coroner will tell us that. Do you know why someone would kill them?"

"Not a clue."

"You're full of shit," he concludes.

"I knew I could count on you to be supportive. I've been through a traumatic experience, and that's your response?"

If he's feeling guilty, he's hiding it well. "You tell me you're involved with Jason Shore, and then from out of nowhere two guys show up dead in the park where you just happen to be walking?"

"I told you about Shore while we were at Charlie's in confidence. . . . You are violating the sports bar privilege. I thought we were french fry blood brothers."

"Don't be a wiseass, Andy. Two people are dead."

"So find out who they are and who killed them. But don't make it my problem, and don't make it about me. I did what any good citizen would do: I reported this. I could have just shut up and let some jogger find them in the morning."

"Why does Shore want you dead? What do you know about him?"

"Not a thing."

"You think this is the only time he is going to come after you?"

"Nobody came after me. I seem to be having trouble explaining that to you."

"You're sticking with that crap?"

"I am sticking to it because it's the truth."

He shakes his head. "Then just be damn careful; I don't want to have to start paying for my own beer."

I decline Pete's offer to send me home in a squad car, which is probably not the smartest thing to do. I just need time by myself to think about things, and I don't want to wait to start.

The lawyer in me is already regretting denying that the dead guys in the park were after me. The truth is that if I could get the jury to know that someone is trying to shut me up, it could redound to the benefit of my client.

But it's too late to change my story, and my reasons for having concocted it remain fairly solid. I'm just thinking that my instinct should have been to put my client first, and it wasn't.

When I get home, I call Laurie, and she answers with "Are you all right?"

"Yes. I assume you know what happened tonight?"

"I do."

"You care to enlighten me?"

"Not over the phone. Get some sleep and I'll be over first thing in the morning."

I understand her reluctance to talk over the phone, so I say good night. However, going to sleep will not be easy; I'm all wound up and the full effects of what happened tonight are starting to hit me.

I pour myself a glass of wine; I would make it Scotch but we don't have any in the house. I sit in the den with the dogs; Tara quickly assumes the position with her head on my lap, so that she can receive petting. Sonny lies on the floor next to us.

"Guys, I'm sorry about tonight. I wish I hadn't exposed you to that."

They don't respond.

"If you're smart, you'll go and live with Nicole."

Laurie is at the house at seven thirty in the morning; she arrives just as I am going out to walk the dogs.

She walks with me, telling me we can talk on the way. Even with her with me, I decide to just walk in the neighborhood and not go back to the park.

I'm glad to get out of the house because the phone hasn't stopped ringing from media people, all of whom I have avoided. Apparently what happened last night is all over the news, and I'm a featured player.

"I assume that was your friend?" I ask. "Or was it you?"

"I really don't want to say anything about that, but I can say that I was not in the park last night."

She doesn't want to throw her colleague under the bus, which I can understand. "Okay, let me tell you what I think happened; if I'm right, blink twice."

She smiles but doesn't say anything.

"I think you were worried about what Shore might do, so you had your friend watching over me. It's why you said he was unavailable the other day. He learned the walk I take every night, and he was in position in case something happened.

"He waited until they were about to kill me and then he acted; he had no choice. He did not want to deal with the police afterwards, so once he knew I was okay, he left and called you."

I look at Laurie and add, "You blinked."

She smiles. "I have something in my eye."

"He's really good at what he does, frightening as that might be." Then, "Do we know if the two dead guys have been identified?"

"They have, but they're hired guns. Doesn't seem like they have any obvious connection to Shore."

We're almost back at the house when I say, "Legally, whoever killed those guys was required to stay and tell the police what happened."

"Yes."

"And you're okay with that not happening?"

"In this case I am, for the same reasons that you are."

"But I don't quite have the ethical boundaries that you do."

"Ethical boundaries are self-imposed; they're whatever you want them to be," she says. Then, "Maybe I'm becoming an 'end justifies the means' person, even though I don't want to see myself that way. It's been an adjustment, but I'm being dragged kicking and screaming in that direction. It's why I've been okay with the hacking work that Sam has been doing."

"You know about that?"

"Duh."

"You saved my life by having me protected."

She shrugs. "Somebody had to. And if I hadn't, I'd be stuck looking for another job."

"Thank you. I'm glad you're smarter than me."

"You're welcome."

We get into the house and I'm about to go into the kitchen to prepare breakfast for the dogs. "You want some coffee?"

Laurie smiles. "You have a coffee machine here?"

"We do. . . . I do."

"Black . . . no sugar."

The phone rings and I yell out, asking her to get it and tell whoever is calling that I'm not doing interviews.

A minute later she comes into the room carrying the phone. "It's Nicole."

I take the phone. "Hello, Nicole."

"Hello, Andy. You and Laurie are getting an early start this morning."

"Yes. Things are heating up . . . on the case." I'm trying to think if I could have used a worse choice of words, but I can't come up with anything.

"I heard on the news that you had some trouble last night. I was just calling to see if you were okay."

"I'm fine."

"Yes, Laurie mentioned that."

"Franklin Lakes is a dangerous community. All I did was take a stroll in the park."

"Be careful, Andy." She hangs up.

That could have gone better.

Neither Laurie nor I say anything about Nicole as we have coffee and the dogs chow down. It's a little awkward and I think we're both feeling it.

I understand Nicole's reaction, even though I have never given her the slightest reason to think I would do anything that I shouldn't.

But I'm also annoyed; she's the one who walked out. On the other hand, she walked out because people are trying to kill me and she is understandably reluctant to get caught in the cross fire. That cross fire was never more evident than last night.

In case you haven't noticed, I'm a little conflicted about this.

Laurie tells me that she has a morning meeting with one of the drivers for Pearson who seemed anxious to talk to her. She asks me if I want to come along.

Might as well.

I don't think it says anything good about me that I just assumed the truck driver we're here to see was a man.

When Heather Tinker invites us into her apartment, I'm expecting her to call her husband to come talk to us. But it turns out that Heather has been driving for Pearson for four years.

"You like working there?" Laurie asks, once we're settled in with coffee. If coffee didn't exist, the number of conversations that take place in the world would be reduced by 70 percent.

"Very much. For the most part it's like a family. But losing Stephen and Denise and Don Muncy . . . it's just so terrible."

"Were you there that night at Morelli's?"

"No; I was on a job. And I'm glad I wasn't. It's hard even to think about. One minute they're having fun, and . . ." Heather doesn't finish the sentence, but it's fairly easy to predict where it would have gone.

"How many days a year are you on the road?" Laurie asks.

"Twenty days a month. It fluctuates, but that's the requirement."

"And do you have a regular route?"

"Not really, although I wind up going to the Midwest a lot. Chicago, St. Louis, Kansas City . . ."

I jump in with a question. "You said before that 'for the

most part' it's like a family at Pearson. What did you mean by that? In what way isn't it like a family."

"Well, a while back they hired a lot of new drivers . . . all men. They are like a separate part of the company; they really don't have much to do with us longtimers. I don't have anything against them; the little interaction I've had with them has been fine. Anyway . . . that's what I meant. They're not part of the Pearson family, at least in my eyes."

"Do they have their own routes?"

"Yes, although we overlap some. They do all the importing and exporting stuff; they're apparently trained in how to navigate the customs situation. And they do some domestic routes as well."

"You don't do any of the importing or exporting work?" I ask.

"No. Which is actually fine with me; I like the longer routes. I'm a loner, I guess."

"Where did the new people come from? Who hired them?"

"I don't really know. It's not like we have an HR department. I guess it was Stephen and Mike Shaffer. They seemed to go on a hiring spree when the company expanded."

"How many drivers are we talking about?" Laurie asks.

"Not sure; maybe ten."

"Do you have any friends at the company that are close with them?" I ask.

"Not really. Like I said, they mostly keep separate."

"Who keeps a record of all the shipments and where they go?" I ask.

"I guess now it's Mike Shaffer, unless he assigned it to someone else. It used to be Ryan; he was like the dispatcher." Then, "I don't think Ryan did what they're saying. I just don't believe it."

"You like Ryan?" Laurie asks.

"Absolutely; he's a good guy."

"Since Stephen Pearson was killed, who has been running the company?"

"From what I can tell, Mike Shaffer. But they don't consult with me, so I could be wrong about that."

"What kind of guy is Shaffer?" Laurie asks.

"This just stays in this room, okay? I need my job."

"You have our word," I say.

Tinker nods. "I don't like him. He's different than Stephen. Stephen would ask about your life, your family, like he really cared. Shaffer treats people like they are just things to be used. It creates a whole different atmosphere."

"Do you know Anna Pearson?"

Tinker shrugs. "I mean, I've met her, but I don't know her that well."

"Has she become active in the business since Stephen died?"

Tinker shakes her head. "Not that I know of. But like I said, they don't talk to me about stuff like that."

"Had she been involved in the company at all, I mean when Stephen was alive?"

"Not that I've seen."

We've gotten all we can from Heather Tinker, and after re-emphasizing that we will keep our conversation confidential, we leave.

Once we're outside, I ask Laurie to find out whatever she can about Anna Pearson.

"You think she's more than just the grieving widow?" Laurie asks.

"I think it's possible."

"Why do you say that?"

"I'm just following the money."

Among the many calls I got the morning after the incident in the park was one from my father.

He was obviously concerned, and while I had reassured him that I was fine, I didn't have much time to chat.

So I'm stopping by today. I haven't seen my father nearly enough lately, partially because I've been busy and partially because I didn't want to get into another conversation about Nicole.

He is outside watering the plants when I arrive. In my entire life I had never seen him water plants. I don't think I'd ever heard him acknowledge the existence of plants.

This is a guy with time on his hands, which I know must be hard on him. Nelson Carpenter, when he was working, filled up every minute of every day. Not anymore, and it is painful for me to see. These plants have been watered so much they're looking like prunes.

"Good-looking garden you got here," I say.

"Yeah. A constant source of excitement for me. Come on in."

We go inside and this becomes the first conversation in three weeks that doesn't take place over coffee. Instead it takes place in front of the television, which is currently showing a taped replay of last night's Yankees-Orioles game. The only thing that interests me less than live Yankee games are taped ones.

"So what happened?" he asks, wasting no time.

"I found two bodies in the park while I was walking the dogs."

"Just like that?"

I nod. "Yup. Wrong place, wrong time."

"You think that just because I spend my day watering plants it means I turned stupid?"

"Okay. They were apparently there to kill me. Somebody stopped them; I don't know who."

"Yes, you do, but don't tell me who it was. Better I don't know. But I do want to know who wanted to kill you and why."

"Do you know Jason Shore?"

"Of course. I served on a charity board with him. He spent his time pretending to know what charity it was. He was known to be 'connected'; is he the one who wants you dead?"

"I can't be one hundred percent sure, but he's definitely the leader in the clubhouse."

"Why?"

"He's involved with Pearson Trucking in a way I don't understand. Apparently he's afraid I will learn to understand it."

"When you worked for those three years as a prosecutor in my office, how many times did people try to kill you?"

"Including blind dates?"

"This is not funny, Andy. Was your life ever in danger?"

"Not that I recall."

"Maybe you made the wrong career move."

"That seems to be the prevailing opinion," I say.

"I assume you're referring to Nicole?"

"Yes."

"But she was okay with things when you were a prosecutor?"

"Yes, but I think that she thought it could lead to me

becoming Senator Carpenter or Governor Carpenter. Or, to quote Michael Corleone, a *pezzanovante*."

"Philip Gant told me he offered you a lucrative position which comes with perks like money, vacations, and nobody taking a shot at you."

"I assume he also told you I turned him down?"

"With extreme prejudice."

"I just can't be a corporate attorney for Philip Gant."

"I understand, believe me. I turned down a similar opportunity multiple times back in the day."

"I never knew that."

He nods. "Probably because I never told you."

"The truth is I don't have to be a defense attorney; there are other things I'd switch to in a minute. But I don't know how to make them happen."

"What would you do?"

"I would happily become the shortstop for the Mets. Or especially quarterback for the Giants; I'd love that, though I'd want them to improve their offensive line."

My father laughs, something he doesn't do that much these days. "You might have trouble pulling that off."

"I know."

"Philip also said Nicole is once again out of the house."

"Yes."

"I think he's getting frustrated with you. Philip hates being frustrated; he finds it frustrating."

"He can join the club. Although, my recollection is that I married Nicole, not Philip. So his frustration is not a cause of great concern for me; Nicole's absence is."

"Andy, what I am about to say should not be considered advice; it's simply a comment."

"Uh-oh."

"You know how much I like Nicole, right?"

"I do."

"Marriage should not be this hard. It certainly wasn't for your mother and me."

"I know. I wish I knew how to make it easier."

"You'll figure it out," he says. "One way or the other."

don't know if Laurie is still having me protectively watched.

I didn't want to ask her because I was afraid it would lead to a conversation in which I would display false bravado and claim I didn't need it. The truth is that I very much need it; the other night proved that rather conclusively.

The good news is that no matter what I said, she would know better. She knows I couldn't begin to take care of myself; she has seen me in action, or inaction, as the case may be.

When I get home, I take the dogs for their walk. I do it when it's still light outside, and I don't go anywhere near the park. I'm nervous about what could happen; if I could send the dogs out to walk themselves, I would do so.

Tara could probably handle it with no problem. I could also send her to the deli to bring in sandwiches, and give her the keys to go gas up the car. She's that smart.

Once we're back, I make myself a sandwich and some french fries. I dunk frozen ones in way too much oil, and some splatters around the kitchen when the fries start to boil. The end product is pretty disgusting, but they are french fries, so of course I eat them. If there is a recommended daily grease allowance, I suck down enough for a couple of months.

My next move is to file a request with the prosecutor's office to receive discovery on the police investigation into the park shooting. My claim is that while I don't know for sure that I was any kind of target, it is certainly possible and justifies my getting the information.

I file the request for two basic reasons. One is that I could learn something that would help me in Ryan's case. The other is that if I find out the police are getting close to what really happened, I can alert Laurie.

I had asked Laurie to find out what she can about Anna Pearson. I will also ask Sam to do the cyber version, but I think I'll fool around with Google on my own for a while.

The more I've thought about it, the more Anna has risen on the list of potential conspirators. I'm not saying that because Stephen was cheating on her; she seemed to have come to terms with that, and I'm sure it had gone on for a long time.

I don't see that as a reason to suddenly blow up his car. Divorce and taking him to the financial cleaners would be a more logical and, on some level, maybe even a more satisfying maneuver.

But if I make the assumption that Shore had Pearson killed, then I need to figure out why, and that's where Anna Pearson enters the picture. Shore needs Pearson Trucking for something; he's not the type to put $2 million into an investment and not want a return.

I'm sure there are numerous reasons Shore could have wanted Stephen Pearson out of the way. Maybe Pearson was balking at what they were doing; maybe he wanted out. Or maybe he wanted more control than Shore was willing to give up.

I don't know the answer to that, but I do know that Shore would not have gotten rid of Stephen without having a plan B in place. Anna would be a logical person to fit that bill.

Mike Shaffer is just an employee; with Pearson out of the way Anna would be the owner. Shore would have had to be confident that he could work effectively with her. He would also have to know that Anna would not hold against him a little thing like blowing up her husband.

So it's off to google Anna Pearson.

The first thing I discover is that Anna did not grow up in poverty. On the contrary, she had what seems to be a more privileged upbringing than Stephen.

She grew up in New York society; her father, since deceased, was a founder and partner at a top Manhattan law firm. Anna went to Sarah Lawrence and got a degree in fine arts there. She even played the role of debutante at some of those New York City balls.

Anna and Stephen were married at the Carlyle, which means it cost a fortune. The wedding announcement was in *The New York Times,* and that had to be because of her. Being the heir to a New Jersey trucking company is not *New York Times* material.

Anna took her fine arts degree and worked in advertising, then briefly in finance. Neither seems to have been an attempt to have a long career in either field, and she was apparently finished with all that working stuff before she was thirty.

Since then she has done whatever it is that Stephen Pearson's wife does, but she has also racked up a lot of charity work. From reading this I doubt she's been filling bowls in soup kitchens; I think she has done it on a higher, more detached level. But she has been on the board of some charities, mostly local.

There's nothing here that is terribly interesting to me, but that is as expected. I doubted she'd have a Wikipedia page that under "Personal Life" would say "participated in the murder of her husband."

I click on images; maybe I'll get to see how Anna looked in her youth in a bathing suit. But there's no such thing; all the photos are of her in evening wear at some gala or another. I hate going to events like that, and it hits me deep in my gut to realize that Nicole would look at the photos with envy.

I'm about to stop when suddenly a photograph just about jumps off the screen at me. It is of Anna at one of those galas, chatting with two men and another woman.

I instantly recognize one of the men. It's not Stephen Pearson. It's Jason Shore.

This sends me back to the main Google page, and I learn that Anna Pearson and Jason Shore were together on the board of a local children's charity, one that runs pre-K and after-school programs.

It's not exactly evidence that they conspired in a murder, but it sure as hell is interesting.

I go back and rerun the same process, seeing if I can connect Stephen Pearson and Jason Shore in a similar fashion. For all I know maybe the couples used to double-date to charity board meetings.

I can't find any connection between the two, though it's possible I'm not looking in the right places. I do not consider myself a professional googler; Sam will probably come up with photos of Shore and Stephen Pearson sharing a hot tub.

But for now I have a link between Anna Pearson, the now sole owner of Pearson Trucking, and Jason Shore, a major and suspicious investor in that same company.

Not a bad night's work.

It beats getting shot at.

I haven't been spending enough time with my client.

I don't need to hold his hand; that doesn't help me advance his case. But I am his main connection to the outside world, and I am definitely the person he is counting on to return him to that world. Therefore, he needs and wants to see me, if for no other reason than to assure him I am hard at work.

The trial is bearing down on us, and I will have to prepare him for what to expect and how to behave. But I don't need to do that today; I'm basically here to keep him calm and to ask a few more questions about Pearson Trucking.

He's also got some questions for me, and the first one is about a subject close to his heart. "How is Sonny doing?"

"He's doing fine; he and Tara are living life without a care."

"You think I'll ever see him again?" It's a creative way to ask his real question, which is *Are we going to win the case?*

"I'm doing my best to make that happen," I say, which is my creative way to say, *I have no idea.*

I move on. "Ryan, somehow Pearson's trucks are being used in a criminal enterprise."

He looks surprised. "What does that mean?"

"I don't know. I was hoping you could tell me."

"I wish I could."

"Could they be shipping illegal goods, like maybe drugs?"

"I guess it's always possible."

"If that were the case, who would be the people that would have to know about it?"

"Mike Shaffer for sure. Maybe Stephen, but . . ."

"Stephen wouldn't be first on that list?"

"No, Stephen really didn't get into the nitty-gritty of things. It's possible Mike could have managed something like that without Stephen knowing."

"Tell me about the new drivers. The ones they hired when the business expanded."

"I really didn't get to know them much; they sort of formed their own group. They weren't unfriendly or anything; the few I talked to seemed like nice guys."

"Why did you have occasion to talk to them?"

"Because I was functioning as a dispatcher. So I'd give them directions; I was trying to make things more efficient. I told you about that."

"Did they follow your directions?"

"I don't know for sure. Basically they just listened and nodded, which is unusual for drivers."

"How so?"

"Drivers have a way of doing things, and they're particular about it. If you tell them A, they say B. I was the same way when I was driving."

"So you as the dispatcher, or anyone at the company, would you have any way of knowing where the trucks were at any one time?"

"Yes."

"How?"

"Two ways. First of all, the drivers would report in and tell us. They are required to do that once a day."

"But they could be lying, right?"

Ryan shrugs. "Always possible. But we also have access to their GPS records; it feeds into the company computers."

"Why?"

"Mostly for insurance purposes. It doesn't only record time and location; it even shows things like the speed at which the trucks are traveling."

"Who would have access to this?"

"Certainly Mike Shaffer, and anybody he delegates with me gone. But it was not something that anyone looked at on a regular basis. There was no reason to think that drivers were lying to us. It was really just for emergencies, or insurance issues."

"Okay. Before I leave, any more questions you have for me?"

"Yeah. Are we ready for the trial?"

"We will be."

"I'm nervous about it," he says.

"Just sit back and watch the show."

"Have you ever done a murder trial before?"

I nod. "Twice."

"How did you do?"

"I won both of them. But—"

He interrupts, "So your clients were acquitted?"

"No, my client was the government. Two guilty verdicts."

"Oh."

I leave the jail and call Sam. He answers on the first ring, as he always does, with "Talk to me."

"Sam, the Pearson trucks are always connected by GPS to the computers in the home office."

"No surprise."

"Maybe not to you; it was to me. Anyway, at any one time the people with access to those computers know where the trucks are, how fast they are traveling, things like that."

"Right."

"Can you get access to those computers?"

"Of course."

"Then do so, please."

I go on to tell him exactly what I want, for now. It will mean waiting a few days, but hopefully it will be worth it.

Now comes the tough part . . . dealing with Laurie. I call her and ask, "What are you doing for dinner?"

There is a pause on the other end, then she says, "I'm going to make an assumption when I answer. I certainly may be wrong, in which case I will have embarrassed myself."

" 'What are you doing for dinner?' didn't strike me as that tough a question."

"That's because you are a man. A married man, and some-one I work for."

"Ah, I understand. How about if I assure you that this din-ner is entirely about work and I will promise to take you to the least romantic restaurant in New Jersey? In fact, I won't even take you; I'll meet you there."

"Okay, then my answer is that I don't currently have plans for dinner."

Laurie is the best-looking person I have ever eaten with at Charlie's Sports Bar.

That's a low bar, since on my previous visits here I ate with Pete Stanton. Laurie could wear a bag over her head and dress up like a refrigerator freezer and she'd be better looking than Pete Stanton.

Pete is not here tonight, which is just as well because he'd probably try to listen in on our conversation. The less cops hear what I'm going to say, the better.

But that's for later. For now I'm enjoying Laurie's company, especially since she has a reasonable understanding of and interest in sports. The Mets game is on, and we both follow it as we talk.

Dinner is almost over when she says, "This was going to be a work dinner. Did I miss that part?"

"No, I've been practicing my speech. It's sort of like an opening and closing argument, in one."

"Uh-oh."

"We are in deep trouble in our case. I have come to believe that Ryan did not commit this crime, but I am nowhere close to proving that. Actually, since I don't have to prove it, I should say that I am nowhere close to demonstrating reasonable doubt as to his guilt.

"So I am going to have to take certain actions that may

backfire or may just get us nowhere, but that I think are necessary to shake things up."

"Okay."

"One of them is to pressure Anna Pearson. I need for her
to make a mistake, and I have a feeling she may not handle
intense stress very well. This is a woman whose biggest decision to date seems to be what to wear to the debutante ball.
I could be wrong about that, and I could certainly be wrong
about her involvement in all this, but if I am, then I haven't
lost anything."

"What do you need me to do?"

"About Anna? Probably nothing."

"Here comes the other shoe." She smiles without any
amusement whatsoever.

I nod. "I believe that the trucks Pearson is using to ship
Jason Shore's merchandise contain illegal contraband of some
kind. I think they are a network that facilitates it getting to
customers all over the country, and the world."

"What do you think it is?"

"I don't know. Maybe drugs, or arms . . . it obviously has
to be something valuable. We know where the trucks are at
any one time, which means we know when they will be un-
guarded."

"How do you know that?"

"There is a GPS system which feeds into their company
computers."

"Sam."

I nod. "Sam." Then, "We need to get into at least one of
those trucks."

"Let me see if I understand this. You are going to illegally
break into a computer system in order to get the information
to allow you to illegally break into trucks?"

"Yes, but I'm going to do it with a great deal of charm."

"Andy—"

I interrupt her, because I can't imagine she will finish the sentence in a way that I will like. "Laurie, when you were a cop, what would you have needed to break into a computer system, or a truck?"

"A warrant signed by a judge."

"And what would that judge have needed to issue that warrant?"

"Come on, Andy, you're a lawyer. You know damn well what—"

I interrupt, "Probable cause of a crime, right? He would want probable cause of a crime."

"Yes." She's getting impatient.

"Well, here in the nonlegal, real world, we have requirements also, and they're not that different. Much less strict . . . that I'll grant you . . . but the 'probable cause' standard works for us also. With a twist."

"A twist?"

"A twist; it's really just semantics, but we change *probable* to *probably,* and then we leave out the judge."

"Are you going to get to the point this decade?" she asks.

"Any minute. I know for a fact that a crime has *probably* been committed. You know it as well; for example, those two guys in the park were obviously in the process of committing a major crime. And we both know that the person behind it was *probably* Jason Shore. We actually exceed the probability standard; it's closer to *definitely.*"

"Andy, the bottom line is that you're asking me to break the law, whatever your rationalizations."

"No, I'm not. I'm not asking you to be involved at all. I'm sorry if I gave you that impression."

"Then why are you telling me this?" She looks around. "Why did you take me to a fancy, romantic dinner?"

"Because I care what you think, and I don't want you to think badly of me. And because if we're working together, there shouldn't be any secrets."

She pauses for a few moments, then smiles. "Well, you're right about one thing: you did do it with a lot of charm."

I return the smile. "I told you so."

"So here's what I won't do, and here's what I'll do. I won't help you break into it. That's a truck too far."

"Understood."

"But I will be there to protect you while you're doing it."

"You don't have to do that. I can handle myself very well when the going gets tough."

"Andy . . ."

"Okay. Protection accepted. Why are you willing to do this?"

She thinks for a moment. "A few reasons. I don't know if Ryan is innocent or not; I'm starting to think there's a chance that he is. But I definitely believe that there is something crooked going on at Pearson Trucking, and I want to see justice prevail there.

"And if they discover you breaking into the truck, they're not going to call the cops; they're going to try and kill you. So by protecting you, I am preventing another crime without participating in one. Does that make sense?"

I smile. "In a rationalization kind of way."

She returns the smile. "That's how it sounded to me too. But I do want to keep you alive. You're my employer and meal ticket."

"My eyes are filling with tears."

I decided to just show up at Anna Pearson's house.

I haven't called first for a number of reasons. One is that it's easier to refuse to see me over the phone; there's a safety in that and an avoidance of confrontation.

Also, if I just show up and she agrees to talk, she hasn't had any time to prepare or anticipate what I am going to ask. That increases the likelihood that she will make a mistake and say something that she'll ultimately regret.

Lastly, there's no downside for me. If she refuses to talk, then she would certainly have refused if I had called. So I haven't lost anything except the time it took to get here.

I ring the bell, and when she comes to the door, I can tell she's surprised. I also think I see a flash of worry, but I could be wrong about that. Maybe it's just wishful thinking.

"Good morning. Sorry to just show up like this, but I have something really important to talk to you about."

"Well, I was just going out, and—"

"This won't take more than ten minutes, and it could be crucial to finding out who planted that bomb in Stephen's car."

She can't look like it's not worth spending ten minutes to help uncover her husband's killer, so I know I have her. "All right. But please make this quick."

We go into the den; this time there is no offer of coffee or anything else. I sit down, but she doesn't. It's her way of showing me that this is going to be a quick meeting; I'm surprised she doesn't take out her car keys.

Since she's in a hurry, I'm going to be considerate and not take the time to tell her that I am wearing a wire. Legally I am not required to notify her; New Jersey is a one-party consent state, and that's true both for phone calls and in-person conversations.

"So you are making progress?" she asks.

"I am. More than I expected, to be honest with you."

"How so?"

"Remember I asked you if you knew Jason Shore, and you said you didn't?"

"Yes."

"And I said he had invested in your husband's company, but you didn't know anything about that?"

"Yes."

"He tried to have me killed the other night. You might have read about it. It was in the park near my house."

"Oh, my. How do you know this?"

"That's not important. But a source very high up in the company has confirmed to me that not only is Jason Shore an investor in Pearson Trucking, but he invested more than two million dollars."

She doesn't know where this is going, so she doesn't want to say anything that will come back to bite her. Instead, she just waits for me to continue.

"Here's the strange thing; actually, two strange things. One is that the company hasn't paid him back anything, not a dime, in the two years since he started making that investment. By the way, my company source tells me that the initial cash infusion was seven hundred and fifty thousand dollars.

"But the other strange thing is that it turns out you do know Jason Shore. You worked with him on a charity board, and I found three photos of you talking with him. Do you want to see them?"

"No. I do know him. Not well, but after you had asked me, I looked him up and it turns out we did work together briefly."

"Ah, that explains it; thanks for clearing that up. Did you then confirm his investment in the company?"

"Yes. And I was assured that it was all done legally and aboveboard."

"That's a relief." I pretend to wipe my brow.

"I don't appreciate your sarcasm, Mr. Carpenter. Are you implying that I have done anything wrong? Because if you are—"

I interrupt, "Not at all. I just thought you claiming not to know someone you knew, or that he was a huge investor in the company you own, was strange. But now it all makes perfect sense."

"Good. Then—"

I interrupt again. "There's just one more thing that I really should point out; you could consider it free legal advice."

"No, thank you. I have better lawyers than you."

"Then you might want to get them ready. But what I wanted to tell you is that you're at a crossroads."

"How is that?"

"You're new to the party. You've been in the background while your husband ran the company. Now you're finding out all these terrible things. If you don't come forward and tell the truth, then you become a part of the conspiracy. If you do, then you're a hero, and the bad guys go to jail."

"Time for you to leave."

"I agree. The next time I see you, you'll be answering all these questions under oath . . . and won't that be fun."

The conversation with Anna Pearson went as well as I had hoped . . . maybe even better.

I got her on tape acknowledging that Jason Shore made a huge investment in Pearson Trucking. Until now I only had two pieces of evidence supporting the existence of that investment. One was that his right-hand man, Kenneth Burks, had repeatedly visited both Stephen Pearson and Mike Shaffer at their offices. I coupled that with Sam's discovering a large investment from an offshore account, and it seemed a logical jump.

The other piece, which was more conclusive in my mind, was the phone call from Shaffer berating me for telling Jason Shore that Shaffer told me about Shore's involvement. Shaffer's call confirmed, at last in my mind, that I was right.

But neither of those things would be admissible in court, which is why my tricking Anna Pearson into admitting the investment is so important. If the judge will let me, I can get her on the stand and confront her with her own voice.

That investment is not of itself illegal; Shore is allowed to invest in any company that will take his money. And it certainly doesn't mean I can get any of it in front of the jury; I haven't come close to connecting it to the car explosion.

But at the very least it brings me a step closer to convincing the judge to subpoena the financial information at Pearson, thereby getting legally what Sam has already uncovered through his hacking.

It won't show Shore's fingerprints, since the money came from a secret account. But with Anna acknowledging the investment on tape, I can make a convincing case that Shore is the source of the money.

One thing has not changed: the key to it all will be discovering, and hopefully exposing, the reason that Shore put all that money into Pearson Trucking.

Sam is working on the truck GPS information, and it's proving more difficult than he expected. But he promises he will get there, and my imploring him to hurry won't help any. He's moving as fast as he can.

We're still going to need to get into the trucks once we establish that one is likely to be carrying the kind of load we're interested in and is parked in a place where we can safely break into it.

To that end I head back to the jail to speak to my client, but first I stop at the office to pick up discovery material that has been sent over. It relates to the police investigation into the shooting in the park.

When I get to the jail, Ryan is once again hopeful that I might be bringing good news, and it always pains me to have to disappoint him.

"I just have a couple of questions for you," I say. "When one of the drivers has a load he's taking somewhere, and he stops overnight, does he sleep in the truck?"

Ryan laughs. "Sleep in the truck? Are you nuts?"

"So where does he sleep?"

"Usually in a roadside hotel, one of those chain places. It goes on the company's dime."

"And they just park in the hotel parking lot?"

"Usually in the back; that's what the hotels insist on. They don't exactly offer valet parking to trucks that size."

"And I assume they're always locked?"

"Of course."

"Not sure how to ask this, but is there any way to pick the locks?"

"You want to break into one?" he asks, clearly surprised.

"Hypothetically."

"Well, I wouldn't know how to do it, if you're talking hypothetically. But if you're talking in the real world, there wouldn't be any need to pick them."

"Why not?"

"Because I have keys to all of them . . . they're in my house."

"Are you serious?"

"Sure. We never wanted to risk losing a key and getting stuck. There's a copy of each one in the office safe, and as the dispatcher I had one as well."

"You, Ryan Tierney, are an outstanding client."

He tells me where the keys are hidden in his house; I'm going to pick them up on the way home. He says that they are listed by license plate, so we shouldn't have any trouble knowing which one is which.

As soon as Sam identifies a truck that we can target and get into, we will go. Unfortunately, it will be during the trial, which is about to start. If there is one thing my law professors were unanimous about, it is never go truck-breaking on a trial night. It takes away from the necessary preparation.

But I'm hoping to break that rule, which I can then add to the list of things I never thought would happen when I decided to become a lawyer. At this point it's a long list. At the top is two guys in the park trying to kill me. Next is a thug breaking into my office intent on breaking my leg.

Truck-breaking is a distant third.

Today I am checking a final box before immersing myself in the trial.

Donald Muncy was the third victim of the car bombing, and my firm assumption is that he was just in the wrong place at the wrong time. Laurie has also been doing some investigating and has assured me there is no reason to think that Muncy was anything other than an innocent bystander, so I was okay with putting this off.

She has performed her magic and gotten Muncy's wife, Sharon, to talk to me. At first Sharon refused, since I am representing the person that she thinks killed her husband. But Laurie was persistent and said Sharon would be available this morning.

Laurie is with me; she felt after talking to her that Sharon would be more comfortable if Laurie came along. We arrive together at the Muncy house, which is a well-kept but modest place in Hawthorne.

Sharon Muncy comes to the door holding a little girl, maybe a year old, in her arms. She smiles at us and invites us in and asks if it would be okay if we talked in the kitchen, and of course we agree.

"I'm sorry the place is such a mess," she says, even though it isn't.

Laurie says, "You should see my house. . . . I aspire to this."

There's actually a playpen set up in what is a fairly large kitchen, and Sharon gently deposits her daughter in it, while handing her toys to play with.

Within moments, coffee is poured and cookies are set out for us, as we sit around the kitchen table. Sharon starts it off by saying, "I know you want to talk about Don."

"Yes," Laurie says. "We know it's difficult and we'll try not to take a lot of your time."

"What is it you want to know?"

"What exactly did Don do at the company?"

"Pretty much everything they asked. Don was amazing with machines, computers, anything technical. He called himself their IT person, but he was more than that."

"Was he always in the main office?" I ask. "He never went on the road?"

"Well, that changed somewhat over time. He was originally strictly in the main office, but gradually he spent more and more time out in Parsippany, at their warehouse."

"Do you know why?" I ask.

"Not really. I just know there was a lot of machinery out there, and I guess they kept all the inventory on computers, so that's where Don was needed. It caused him to keep crazy hours, but they paid him fairly well."

"He worked a lot of overtime?" I ask. None of this is necessarily interesting to us; we're just trying to ease our way into talk of her husband's death.

"Oh, yes."

"So he liked working for the company?"

"He certainly did for a long time, but that changed recently. He was actually talking about quitting. He said the hours and the responsibilities were causing him too much stress."

"That surprised you?" I ask.

"Very much. But if Don were here now, he would certainly want to leave. He'd be very angry."

"Why?"

"Employees were told that the company took out life insurance policies as a perk. . . . The amount was supposed to be five times their salary. But I found out they never did that."

"Who told you that?"

"Mr. Shaffer. It's money we . . . I . . . was counting on. He told me if I wanted, he could find work for me there. I told him about our child, and that I needed to take care of her, but he said that wasn't his problem."

"I'm sorry to hear that," Laurie says.

Sharon nods. "Me too."

Time to bite the bullet. "We don't think Don was in any way a target, but we're just covering all our bases. Did he have any enemies within the company that you know of? Or outside the company?"

She shakes her head vigorously. "Absolutely not. Everyone loved Don."

"That's what everyone has told us," Laurie says.

"Thank you," I say. "We appreciate the time."

There is a long list of legal firsts for me on this case, simply because I have switched sides and am handling the defense.

Today's jury selection is the latest example.

I've done jury selection from the prosecution side on quite a few occasions, but this is different. The prosecution always assumes, usually correctly, that theirs is a powerful, compelling case. They would not have brought it if they thought otherwise.

They therefore believe that the majority of the jurors will ultimately come down on the side of conviction. But a majority is not enough for them, at least not in a criminal trial. They have to have unanimity; all twelve jurors have to ultimately vote in lockstep.

On the defense side, my side, we have a different goal. Acquittal would be wonderful, but the more realistic hoped-for outcome is the lack of a conviction. A hung jury works just fine; then it's up to the prosecution to decide whether it's worth retrying the case. And if they do, then another hung jury remains the goal.

So while the prosecution is longing for people who will collaborate and strive to come to a collective decision, we on the defense side are looking for an independent thinker, someone courageous and strong-willed enough to stand on his or her own.

Those kind of people are rare, at least in the real-life world of a courthouse and jury room. There is intense pressure on the one or two people that might stand in the way of a consensus, and even those that claim they could hang tough often eventually buckle under.

But the one common thread that weaves its way through both sides is that none of us have a clue. This is partly because prospective jurors in voir dire are putting on a show.

They want to project an image of themselves that may or may not be true, and we just don't know them well enough to have any idea if they are as they represent themselves.

Additionally, some of them want to be on the jury and some don't. So they will answer questions in a way that they think will accomplish their goal.

There is considerable media interest in this case, and the press is well represented in the gallery today. That will only make the prospective jurors less likely to act and speak normally.

The prosecution employs jury selection experts and I don't. It's not that I can't afford it; the public defender budget provides for it. It's more that I think my gut instincts are as good as theirs, and to be honest, mine aren't any good.

Judge Alan Brickman is in charge, and he is known for moving trials along at what could be described as legal warp speed. Of course, legal warp speed is still slow by real-world standards, but Judge Brickman does what he can.

Because of his efforts, we are able to get the whole thing done by midafternoon. We wind up with seven women and five men. It's an ethnic mixture and probably accurately represents Paterson's diverse population.

I'm satisfied with our panel, but I refer you to my comment about not having a clue.

"How did we do?" Ryan asks, when the final juror is in place.

"I'll let you know when the verdict comes in."

I've told Ryan to remain impassive, to show no emotion one way or the other throughout the trial. He's doing that today, but I have a feeling he's actually enjoying the process.

After all those days dealing with the monotony and loneliness of jail, people are finally paying attention to him. Of course, almost all those people are intent on putting him away for the rest of his life, but at least he feels like he has a chance.

He hasn't asked me what our chances are; I think he knows he won't like the answer. And it wouldn't matter what I say. This trial is going to run its course, and then it will be up to the jury we just picked.

Judge Brickman annoys me by saying that there is enough time for Karen Vincent to deliver the prosecution's opening argument, after we take a quick break. The judge seems to believe that courtroom hours are a precious commodity and that it's a mortal sin to waste them.

The net effect of all this is that Vincent will be able to tell the jury why they should convict Ryan of this terrible crime, and I won't be able to rebut it until tomorrow. The jury will therefore spend the crucial first night having heard only one side of the argument.

During the break I receive a message from Sam telling me he has some interesting information for me. I call back and ask that he come to the house tonight, and then I call Laurie to ask her to come as well. She doesn't answer the phone, so I leave a message.

There's also a message from Nicole, wishing me luck on the trial. Then she closes with "I miss you, Andy, but you understand. . . ."

Actually, I don't.

Or maybe I do.

Vincent stands looking confident, which is probably because she is confident. She smiles at the jury, making an immediate connection. I had heard she was good and I'm afraid I am about to get confirmation of that rumor.

"Well, here we go" is how she starts. "Ladies and gentlemen, you are in the process of taking on an awesome responsibility. Three people are dead, the victims of what I'm sure Mr. Carpenter would agree is an absolutely horrible crime.

"Where we disagree is on who committed it. The State of New Jersey, which I represent, believes the guilty party to be Ryan Tierney. Most important, we believe we can and will prove it.

"Judge Brickman will certainly tell you this, but that proof must be beyond a reasonable doubt. That's a heavy burden, as it should be. If you are going to convict Mr. Tierney of this offense, you must be sure. But we would not be here, Mr. Tierney would not be sitting there, if we did not think we could meet that burden.

"So while your job is difficult in its importance, it's rather simple in its execution. What you must do, the only thing you must do, is follow the evidence. Not what we lawyers say, not even what I am saying now, but the evidence that we will present during the course of this trial.

"Let me briefly describe the facts as you will hear them. Three people died in a car explosion. Their names are Stephen Pearson, Denise Clemons, and Donald Muncy. All three worked at a company that Stephen Pearson owned called Pearson Trucking.

"Ryan Tierney also worked there; he and Stephen Pearson knew each other since childhood. But Stephen Pearson fired Ryan Tierney, and Mr. Tierney was upset about it. He threatened Mr. Pearson, and two weeks later Mr. Pearson was dead.

"There was a company party thrown by Mr. Pearson at Morelli's Restaurant. It was a twice-a-year event to show appreciation to the employees for their hard work. Mr. Tierney was not there because he had been fired.

"We will show that Mr. Tierney came to that neighborhood that night; he accidentally left a calling card to prove it. We will show that Mr. Tierney was an expert in the type of explosives that were used, and that he had some in his basement.

"So he had the motive, and the opportunity, and the expertise. In tennis, we would call that game, set, and match.

"Let me talk to you for a bit about circumstantial evidence. You'll notice that I did not tell you that anyone saw Mr. Tierney plant the bomb. There was no eyewitness to the event; there rarely is. That's because people who commit crimes, who commit murder, like to do it secretly. Makes sense, right?

"But circumstantial evidence is very often far more reliable than eyewitness testimony. The old example, and forgive me if you've heard it before, but it's still the best one, is this. . . .

"You go to sleep and there is no snow on the ground. You wake up in the morning and there are ten inches of the white stuff everywhere, and you need to be plowed to get out of your driveway.

"You didn't see it snow. You were not an eyewitness to it snowing. But you know damn well that it snowed, and you know it beyond a reasonable doubt. And how do you know it? Through circumstantial evidence.

"So that's what you're going to hear from our witnesses, and from our scientists. No eyewitnesses, but proof beyond a reasonable doubt.

"All I ask is that you follow the evidence."

Getting into one of these trucks is not going to be easy," Sam says.

Sam has come to the house this evening to update me on his progress, and I've delayed planning my opening statement to hear what he has to say. But as opening sentences go, this is not a good one.

He continues, "As you might expect, they don't really stop for the night in this area. If they are going to the warehouse in Parsippany, then there's no reason to stop close by; they might as well finish the trip.

"If they're leaving the warehouse, then they also wouldn't stop to spend the night close by; they might as well leave in the morning. These are just my suppositions, but they're based on the GPS data I'm seeing."

"This is not what I wanted to hear, Sam," I say, and Laurie nods slightly in agreement, or sympathy.

"It gets better," Sam says. "There's a diner about ten miles from the factory where they almost always stop to eat in the evening on the way in to the warehouse. They also stop there in the morning for breakfast on the way out, but that's not as regular.

"I assume that when they get to the warehouse at night, they will have to help unload their cargo, and they'd want to have dinner first."

"So we need to check out the diner," I say.

Sam nods. "I already did. They park in the back and are usually in the diner for at least forty-five minutes. Since it's dark at that hour, I think we can get in and out without being seen."

"Is it the same time each evening?"

"No, and it's not every evening. But using the GPS data as it comes in, I can tell when a truck is heading in that direction, and we'd have time to go meet it if they are hungry and stop."

"Okay, so we start tomorrow night. Laurie, are you good with that?"

"I am," she says. "But I'm not sure this is necessary."

"What do you mean?" I ask.

"Let Sam finish and then I'll explain."

"Okay, there's one other thing," Sam says. "Though I'm not sure what to make of it. Sometimes the trucks don't go where they are supposed to."

"How's that?" I ask.

"Well, I'll give you an example. A truck was moving a family from Detroit to New Jersey. So they sent a truck out to an address to pick up the stuff."

"And?"

"And the address was fake and the family doesn't exist, at least not that I can find. I checked because I noticed that the truck didn't go to Detroit like the computer log said; it went to a steel mill near Pittsburgh."

"Does this happen often?"

"I found two examples of it, and I'm sure there must be more."

"In those two cases, were the drivers from the new group that was brought in?"

He shrugs. "I don't know who is part of that group. I guess I can access the personnel records and try to figure it out."

We kick the situation around awhile, but none of us can figure out what is going on. Then I ask Laurie to explain her comment that entering the trucks might not be necessary.

"I've been out at the warehouse for the last two days."

"Inside?" I ask.

"No, watching from a distance, but able to see every truck that arrived and departed."

"What did you learn?"

"That each truck going in either direction, to or from the warehouse, was a Pearson truck."

"Why does that surprise you?"

"Because if they are distributing products, then you would think the manufacturers of those products would be using their own trucks to bring them the merchandise. That would happen at least some of the time, but in these two days, not at all.

"A truck would come in, maybe with a load, maybe not. There's no way for me to know. The same truck would usually depart hours later. So they were either dropping off or picking up, or more likely both."

"So why don't we need to break into one?"

"We . . . I should say you . . . might need to do it. That remains to be seen. But the trucks all load and unload at a huge loading dock in the back. The stuff is put on pallets and then brought inside or outside on forklifts. If we can get close enough, and I think we can, we might be able to see what the products are. That's if they are correctly marked."

"Do some come in after dark?" Sam asks.

"I don't know. I haven't been there at night."

Sam seems invigorated. "I can go out there with night-vision glasses and telescopic lenses. It will be easy."

"And dangerous," I say.

"I'm on the case." Sam is clearly overconfident. "But if it doesn't work, we can always break into the trucks."

I nod. "Sounds like a plan. Anybody have anything else?" When there is no response, I add, "Since no one has anything more to add, I suggest we adjourn the meeting."

But first I tell Sam I want to show him something. I get the discovery documents from the park shooting from my office and show him the specific reference I'm interested in. "According to the police investigation, each of the guys in the park had twenty-five grand wired to them three days before they died. Is there any way to tell who sent it?"

He looks at the information. "Not for certain, but I'd bet that I know."

"How?"

"These are from an untraceable account in the Caymans, but see here? They have a code number, which means nothing to us, but everything to the bank."

"And?"

"And I'll have to check, but I'd be willing to bet that's the same code as the two million wired to Pearson Trucking. If Jason Shore was responsible for sending that other money, then he sent this as well."

"Which means he's made his first mistake," I say. "Hopefully the first of many."

Sam leaves and I mention to Laurie that I'm going to walk the dogs.

"I'll go with you. I could use a walk myself, but you can handle the plastic bag."

"It's dark out, so you're making sure I don't get killed?"

She smiles. "You read my mind."

We go for the walk and I would be lying to myself if I

didn't admit that it is nice being with Laurie. But the truth is that being so comfortable with Laurie is making me uncomfortable. I am attracted to her, maybe because I'm angry with Nicole, or maybe not.

If you hooked me up to a lie detector and asked if I loved Nicole, I would say yes and the machine would confirm it. But does my reaction to Laurie indicate the opposite or at least call it into question?

Either way I am not going to pursue anything with Laurie, which is just as well, because I'm sure I would be rebuffed if I tried.

We get back and Laurie leaves. Ten minutes later the doorbell rings. I turn on the outside light and see that it's Laurie. Maybe she is having the same feelings that I am?

She's not.

As soon as I open the door, she says, "Mike Shaffer is dead. I just heard it on the radio."

"What happened?"

"He was shot in his office tonight. They're calling it a robbery gone bad."

"They didn't catch the shooter?"

"Apparently not."

I think about it for a moment and then say what we're both thinking. "I got him killed."

Last night Laurie tried to reassure me that I was not responsible for Mike Shaffer's death.

She had come in after telling me the news, and we sat on the couch in the den, drinking wine. She was clearly attempting to comfort me because she thought I was upset thinking that I cost a man his life.

I wasn't. She obviously thinks I am a better, more caring person than I am. So I set her straight: "Whatever is going on, Shaffer was neck-deep in it. So was Pearson, but they somehow both became a threat, so Shore and his people got rid of both of them."

"You don't know that."

"Of course not; I don't know anything. It's a theory."

"So continue on with your theory."

"They were able to get rid of Pearson because they had Shaffer. Then they got rid of Shaffer because they have Anna Pearson. She will install whoever they want in Shaffer's slot, and business will continue as usual."

"And you think they killed Shaffer because you told Shore that Shaffer told you about his investment in the company?"

"I think that started the process. Then I told Anna Pearson that someone in the company had revealed more, like the fact that the debt to Shore had never been repaid. I didn't mention Shaffer by name and didn't really intend to give her that impression, but she likely assumed that there was no one else that could have provided the information."

"So you're not feeling guilty?"

I smile. "Are you kidding? I'm feeling all-powerful. Now I have to find a way to use what happened tonight to my client's advantage."

She returns the smile. "And here I thought you had a conscience."

"I cut class the day they taught conscience in law school."

Laurie leaves and I lock the door behind her and get ready for bed. I have to go over in my mind what I am going to say in court tomorrow, but I can do that with my head on the pillow. I don't want to memorize or write out what I am going to say; I think it will be more effective if I do it spontaneously, within guidelines.

When I get into bed, Tara jumps in as well and lays her head on my chest. It's the first time she has done this, and it makes me feel good that she must be feeling completely comfortable and at home.

I walk the dogs in the morning and head for the courthouse. I arrive about a half hour early, which gives me some time to calm my nerves. I'm not sure why, but sitting at the defense table in a mostly empty courtroom tends to relax me and lets me clear my mind.

I also have some time to talk to Ryan and tell him about Shaffer's death, which shocks him. He asks what effect that might have on our case, but I don't give him a clear answer because I don't have one.

Judge Brickman is prompt as always, calls the jury in, and tells me that the floor is mine.

"Ladies and gentlemen, first of all I want to thank you for serving. You have an extremely important job, and you're going to have to do it under great pressure. The life of this man, Ryan Tierney, is in your hands, and all I ask is that you follow your instincts, and, yes, the evidence, and do what you think is right and fair.

"Ms. Vincent talked to you about circumstantial evidence, and most of what she said is true. Eyewitness evidence of a crime like this is rarely available, and not always reliable. So that leaves circumstantial evidence, and that's what we have here.

"But your job is not to figure out if it snowed last night; that's an easy one. Let's try rain. Suppose you went to sleep and the street outside your window was dry, but when you woke up, it was wet.

"Did it rain? Circumstantial evidence would say yes. But what if just before you woke up, a street cleaner had come along and spread water on the pavement? It's still circumstantial evidence, but it is evidence that was, in effect, planted.

"So while the evidence is important and should be respected and analyzed, it is vitally important to know the source.

"Ryan Tierney has never been accused of a crime in his life . . . not once. Nor has he ever committed one. He served with distinction as a marine and had a tour of duty in Iraq.

"He was a faithful employee of Pearson Trucking, and then one day he was fired, without cause. He was told that it was for financial reasons, that the company was doing badly. He knew that was not true, and it made him upset.

"Have any of you ever been let go from a job or know someone who that happened to? It is upsetting, and it can make one angry, especially if it's unjustified. But did you ever kill three people because of it? Did anyone you know ever blow up a car?

"There is an explanation for everything Ms. Vincent is going to tell you. You don't have to believe the explanations to acquit Ryan Tierney, though I hope and think that you will believe them. But that is not the requirement. The only way you can convict is if you think our explanations are absolutely wrong, wrong beyond a reasonable doubt.

"There are criminal activities going on at Pearson Trucking. The people behind it all decided that Stephen Pearson had to go, he was in their way, and that Ryan Tierney was in the perfect position to take the fall.

"You will hear all about it, then you will deliberate and render your best judgment. That's all I or anyone else can ask of you.

"Thank you."

I go back to the defense table and exhale for the first time in what feels like a week. I look at the jury, maybe hoping that they'll give me a standing ovation, but they're impassive.

Ryan tells me that I did great. My client, who is facing life in prison, is trying to cheer me up.

We jump right in, since Judge Brickman doesn't waste any time, and Karen Vincent's first witness is Joseph Morelli, the owner of the restaurant where the party was the night of the explosion.

I met Morelli when I visited the scene and he was still dealing with the destruction of his business. My understanding is that the rebuilding is almost finished.

"And you are the owner of Morelli's Restaurant?" she asks.

"Along with my brother, Tommy, yes. We're partners."

"How long have you owned it?"

"My father opened the restaurant thirty-one years ago."

She quickly brings him to the night of the explosion. "You were there at the Pearson Trucking party?"

"Yes, they took over the restaurant. They've been doing this twice a year for as long as I remember. I'm at the restaurant almost every night, and that day was no exception."

"Did anything unusual happen that night?" She realizes that can be considered a ridiculous question, so she corrects herself. "I mean during the party itself."

"No, or at least not that I saw. Everybody seemed to be having a great time."

"A lot of drinking?"

"No more than usual, but certainly some people were drinking."

"What time did it end?"

"It started breaking up at about ten thirty."

"Who were the last to leave?"

"Stephen Pearson always waited until the end to drive home whoever might have had too much to drink. In this case he left with Denise Clemons and Donald Muncy."

"They had consumed a lot of alcohol?"

"If they had, I couldn't tell. They seemed okay to me. Donald might have acted a little tipsy. But I really didn't pay much attention because Stephen was in charge."

"So when they left, you were the only person still in the restaurant?"

"Yes, I was closing up."

"And their car was in the parking lot in the rear?"

"Yes."

Vincent shows him photographs of the back area that Morelli must have supplied because they were taken before that night. She asks him to point out where the car was, and he does so. She then asks what happened next.

"I heard this incredibly loud noise, and the whole building shook. I was in the front, and it felt like I was in an earthquake. It literally knocked me over."

"What did you do next?"

"I went into the back. The entire building had been blown open, and then I saw the car. . . . It was horrible. . . . It was still burning. It wasn't even a car anymore."

That leads to the highlight of the testimony, at least from Vincent's point of view. She is able to introduce photos of the devastation, making sure that the jury sees multiple views of the horror. When they are sufficiently outraged and repulsed, she turns the witness over to me.

"Mr. Morelli, throughout the party itself, it seemed to be going well?" I ask.

"Yes."

"No one seemed upset, at least not that you noticed?"

"No."

"You spoke to Mr. Pearson that night?"

"Yes."

"Did you notice anything unusual about him, his mood? Did he seem afraid of anything?"

"No."

"He seemed to be having fun?"

"Yes."

"Did he mention anything about being threatened?"

"No . . . not to me."

"Do you have any information, anything at all, which can help inform this jury as to who might have been responsible for the explosion?"

"No, I don't."

"Thank you."

Next up for the prosecution is Medical Examiner Janet Carlson.

I've worked with Janet a number of times in my previous life; she is competent at what she does and is also an extremely effective witness.

She is also attractive, with an engaging smile; if you saw her, you could make a thousand guesses at her occupation before you came to "person who cuts up dead bodies."

Janet's medical expertise is not what is important to Karen Vincent right now. When three people are blown to bits in an explosion, cause of death is not that difficult to determine. For example, one could quickly rule out natural causes.

Vincent's goal is to have a reason to once again trot out the horrible photos and to couple it with an even more horrible verbal description of the carnage.

After showing the photos again, Vincent asks Janet if she conducted the autopsies on the victims.

"I did not," Janet says. "The bodies were not in a condition for autopsies to be conducted. They were not in any way intact, and the fire further contributed to the situation."

"How did you identify them?"

"Through DNA, supported by the testimony of Mr. Morelli as to who was in the car. We didn't actually know who the victims were until early the following morning."

"In your experience, have you ever dealt with bodies so horribly damaged?"

"I have not."

Vincent turns the witness over to me, knowing full well that there is nothing for me to get from her. Basically I just want to get her off the stand so the jury might stop thinking about bodies that are so mutilated that they can't even be autopsied.

"So you did not conduct autopsies on the deceased?" I ask.

"I did not."

"Therefore you did not determine a cause of death?"

"Not officially, no."

"You are here as a medical examiner, an expert in your field. Was any of your medical training helpful in your testimony today?"

"What do you mean?"

"If you hadn't had all that training, would your testimony today have been any different?"

"Not really, no."

"So would it be a fair summation of your testimony to say that you told this jury that three people who were obviously killed in an explosion were killed in an explosion?"

She smiles. "That would be fair, yes."

"Is there anything about the work you did on this case that gives you any idea who might have committed the crime?"

"No."

"Why are you here?" I ask, a question she had probably never before been asked.

"I was summoned to testify, and it's my job to do so."

"Do you think you were summoned so the jury would be forced to hear and see more of the horrors of this crime? So that it might anger them?"

Karen Vincent jumps out of her seat with an objection, and Judge Brickman instantly sustains it. "Be careful, Mr. Carpenter, I will not tolerate that in my courtroom."

"My apologies, Your Honor," I say, with a total lack of sincerity. I then turn to Janet, who is having trouble concealing a smile. She knows I was absolutely correct in my assessment and is probably annoyed with being used like this. "Thank you . . . no further questions."

It has not been a devastating day; no one has yet connected Ryan to the crime, though Vincent had not intended to do that through these witnesses. Worse days are to come.

I head home to walk the dogs and then wait for Sam and Laurie to come over. Sam has a report to give us on his nighttime observations of the warehouse in Parsippany.

I'm conducting most of these meetings at home, especially now that we are holding them at night in deference to the daytime court sessions. There seems to be no reason to trek down to the office; it's much more comfortable at home, and it means the dogs are left alone for less time.

Besides, I haven't gotten around to getting that damn coffee machine, and it's embarrassing.

Once Sam and Laurie are here and settled in, Sam says, "What I saw is not what I expected. In terms of what came in to the warehouse on the trucks, there were obviously a lot of large boxes, but it is impossible to know what was in them. They were not marked in any way, which by itself is surprising.

"But then there were these huge, flat cartons, so wide that they barely fit in the trucks. And they appeared to be extremely heavy. . . . It took two forklifts to take them out of the trucks and into the warehouse. Again, I have no idea what that was. Could have been wood, metal, plastics . . . there is just no way to know."

"So we're nowhere," I say.

"We're certainly not where we want to be," Laurie adds, and Sam doesn't disagree.

"But there is one strange thing," Sam says. "There is tremendous activity there at night, and it's all concentrated in one area of the warehouse, which probably occupies a third of the total building. The lights are on there, but the rest of the place is dark."

"Maybe it's different during the day," I say.

"I don't think so. I got there today at about four o'clock and went up to the front entrance and rang the bell."

"What?" I ask, even though I heard him.

"I figured, what could go wrong? It was broad daylight, and they would have no idea who I am."

"What happened?"

"A guy comes to the door, and I pretended I was looking for work. I said I worked in warehouses all the time, knew how to handle the machines, stuff like that."

"He said they weren't looking for anyone and blew me off, so I left."

"Did you learn anything?" Laurie asks.

He nods. "The place is empty, or almost empty. I'm talking about a huge area, the same part where I did not detect any action at night. Whatever is going on there, whatever they are doing or storing, it's taking place in that one-third of the building that is lit up at night."

"Anyone have an explanation for this?" I ask, but no one volunteers.

"Okay, we're back to planning a break-in into a truck."

T racy Murch works in the accounting department at
Pearson Trucking.

Vincent gets her to describe what she does, then asks her
where her cubicle was located in the office. Vincent shows her
a diagram of the place to help the jury understand.

"My desk was right here." Murch points.

"How far would you say that is from Stephen Pearson's
office?"

Murch points again. "This is . . . this was . . . his office."

"And the exterior was glass? So you could see in?"

"Yes."

"Could you often hear what was being said in there?"

"Only if the people were speaking loudly. And Stephen . . .
Mr. Pearson . . . rarely yelled."

"A couple of weeks before Stephen Pearson died, did he
meet in his office with Ryan Tierney?"

"Yes."

"And were you at your desk at the time?"

"Yes, I was."

"Please describe what you saw and heard."

"I saw Ryan . . . Mr. Tierney go in and close the door. Then,
maybe a minute or two later, I heard yelling."

"Who was doing the yelling?"

"Mr. Tierney."

"What did he say?"

"'How could you do this, Stephen? What the hell are you doing?' I can't be sure those were the exact words, but it's close. Mr. Tierney was leaning over the desk, with his face close to Mr. Pearson's."

"And what was Mr. Pearson saying in response?"

"I don't know; he wasn't yelling. But he did not look happy."

"How long did this go on?"

"Just a couple of minutes. Everybody in the office was watching and listening to it. We were all shocked because Stephen and Ryan always seemed to be good friends."

"Did Mr. Tierney say anything else that you could hear?"

"Yes. He screamed, 'You are going to regret this, Stephen. I swear to God, you are going to regret this.'"

"Did Mr. Tierney eventually leave the office before Stephen?"

"Yes. He slammed the door behind him, and then I guess he saw that everyone was staring at him, so he said, 'I got fired! Do you believe that? I got f-ing fired.'"

"Did he say 'f-ing'?"

"No, he said the whole word."

It's my turn to question Murch, and there's not a lot for me to get from her. I'm sure she accurately described what she heard and saw.

"Ms. Murch, do you know Ryan Tierney?"

"Oh, yes."

"You like him?"

"Yes."

"Consider him a friend?"

"Yes." Then, "I hope this doesn't change that."

I smile. "You're just telling the truth as you know it."

"Thank you."

"Have you ever known Mr. Tierney to be violent?"

"No."

"Did Mr. Tierney leave the office entirely after he left Mr. Pearson's office?"

"Yes. I mean, I didn't see him again that day."

"Did you and some of the other people in the office discuss what you had all witnessed?"

"Yes."

"Can you briefly describe what those conversations were like?"

"We were just all shocked and didn't understand why Ryan would be fired like that. It seemed so sudden and out of left field."

"Didn't anyone suggest calling the police?"

"No. Why would we do that?"

"You said that Mr. Tierney threatened and warned Mr. Pearson."

"Well, yes, but we didn't think we should call the police over that. No one felt that Ryan would do anything."

"So you and your friends were not worried that Mr. Tierney would do anything violent?"

"Nobody said anything like that."

"Thank you."

Judge Brickman adjourns court for the day. I haven't mentioned anything about Shaffer's death; I need to use it strategically to make sure it's admissible.

I head for my car. On the way I check my voice messages; since I have to have my phone off all day, I always check it immediately in case Sam or Laurie is calling with any important developments.

The voice I hear is neither Sam's nor Laurie's, but I do

recognize it. "Mr. Carpenter, this is Randy Clemons . . . Denise's husband. You said to call if I had anything to talk to you about. . . . Well, I have something to talk to you about. Please call me back."

So that's what I do; I call him back and he immediately says he has something important for me. "Can we meet tonight?" he asks.

"If it's that important."

"That will be for you to judge. I just want to say what I have to say before I change my mind."

"So we'll meet tonight."

tell Clemons to be at my office at seven thirty and then call Laurie and Sam to tell them that our meeting for tonight is off.

When Laurie hears the reason, she asks to be included in the meeting with Clemons.

"You think he's going to shoot me? He's an ex-cop."

"I don't know him."

"That's because he was in Clifton PD."

"Good, we can swap cop stories."

"I didn't hire you as a bodyguard, Laurie."

I can almost see her smiling through the phone. "I know; I'm throwing that in for free."

I arrive at the office at ten after seven and Laurie gets here ten minutes later. "Let's have some coffee while we wait," she says, knowing it's not possible.

"About that . . ." Then I am mercifully interrupted by the arrival of Clemons.

He walks in and looks around. "This is your office?"

"It is. And this is my associate Laurie Collins. Laurie, Randy Clemons."

They shake hands and we all sit down. I sit at my desk, Laurie on the only chair, and Clemons on the couch. "What did you want to tell me?" I ask.

"About two weeks before she died, Denise told me that Stephen Pearson was worried."

"About what?"

"He was afraid of Jason Shore. He told her there was a problem between them, and there was no telling what Shore might do."

"Did she say what the problem was?"

"No."

"What else did she say?"

"That Shore is the one who told Stephen to fire Ryan Tierney."

"Did she say why?"

"No, and I didn't ask. I really didn't know Tierney . . . maybe spoke to him once."

"What else did she say about Shore? I don't just mean at that time, I mean at any point over the last couple of years."

"Just that Shore bailed them out financially. She said Pearson didn't want to get in bed with him, but that he had no choice."

"I saw you twice and both times I asked you if your wife had ever said anything like this, and both times you said no."

He nods uncomfortably. "I know. It was a mistake."

"It wasn't just a mistake. It was a lie. Why did you do it?"

"Because as you can imagine, I had been following the case, and I was sure Tierney had done it. With him knowing about explosives, and his car getting a ticket . . . it just seemed like a slam dunk."

Clemons is quiet for a few seconds, then continues, "So even though she had said what she said, I was afraid that if I revealed it, it might deflect away from Tierney. If he killed Denise, and I thought he did, there was no way I could live with myself if I helped get him off."

"So what made you come forward now?" I ask. Laurie hasn't said a word since the conversation turned to the case.

"Mostly Mike Shaffer . . . I mean, his getting killed. I'm a cop; I don't believe in coincidences, at least not that big. Two executives of the same company to get targeted and killed—after what Denise said, I just couldn't keep quiet about it anymore.

"I still don't know for sure what the truth is, but I felt I needed to get the facts out there and let the chips fall where they may."

"Will you testify to this?"

He nods. "I wouldn't look forward to it, but I'm in all the way."

I would turn cartwheels right now if I were alone and if I were capable of turning a cartwheel. An ex-cop, lost a leg in the line of duty, widowed in the crime the jury is considering . . . it would be hard to find a more credible and sympathetic witness.

"Okay, you did the right thing, albeit a little late. I'll let you know when I'm going to need you."

When he leaves, I ask Laurie, "Do you believe him?"

"That depends. Does he have any reason to lie?"

"Not that I can see."

"Then I believe him."

I nod. "Me too."

Angela Brock is the officer who wrote the ticket that placed Ryan's car near Morelli's.

The car was parked directly in front of a fire hydrant; and the ticket places the car at a time when the party was in progress.

After establishing Brock's job and her responsibilities, Vincent asks, "Do you generally make the rounds in this area every night? Is that a specific area that you always cover?"

"Yes. I'm on five nights a week; I'm off Mondays and Tuesdays, and I work from four to midnight."

"Do you give out a lot of tickets?"

"Maybe forty a night, on average, but most come between four and six o'clock, since after that parking is generally allowed."

"But parking next to a fire hydrant is never allowed?"

"That's correct."

"So how did you happen to ticket this particular car?"

"We have a Parking Violations Bureau number that people can call and report something that they see. We got a call about this car, and the message was forwarded on to me. I then went there and ticketed the car."

Vincent introduces photos of the car where it was parked that night, taken from a number of different angles, and Brock confirms they are the ones she took.

"Why do you take the photos?"

"In case the owner disputes the ticket in court."

"Do you ever tow away cars that are illegally parked in this area?"

"No, not unless they are blocking traffic."

Vincent then introduces the photos of Ryan's car, taken in his driveway the next morning. Like the photos of the car by the hydrant, I have also seen these in the discovery.

The judge asks if I have an objection to the introduction of the driveway shots. Since Brock didn't take them, I could insist that the person who did take them testify to it.

"No objection, Your Honor." What Vincent does not realize is that I am extremely anxious for these photos to be admitted, so I would not dream of delaying that process.

Vincent painstakingly takes Brock through a process to show the jury that the two sets of photos show the same car. It is the same make, model, and color and, most significant, has the same license plate number.

"Is there any doubt in your mind that all these photographs are of the same car?"

"No doubt at all," Brock says.

"Did I ask you to do a computer search to determine who this car and license plate is registered to?"

"You did. It is Ryan Tierney's car."

"Thank you."

I get up to question Officer Brock, and my only concern is that I may be salivating.

"Officer Brock, who called the Parking Bureau to report this violation?"

"I don't know; they didn't tell me."

"Okay, we'll get to that later in the trial. Now, I have taken the liberty of enlarging two photographs, and I'd like you to confirm that they are identical to the ones you just analyzed."

I take out two Styrofoam boards with the blown-up photos, one taken in front of the hydrant, and one in Ryan's driveway. In both cases the photo was taken from the rear.

She confirms that they're the same, and Vincent has no objection, so they are admitted into evidence.

"If in the process of giving a ticket for a violation, do you look for other violations? Like an overdue inspection, broken taillight, anything like that?"

"Yes."

"Looking at this photo of the car parked in front of the hydrant, do you see any other violation that you should have ticketed for?"

She spends a significant amount of time looking at it, probably because she is concerned that I am trying to trick her. Finally she says, "I don't see anything."

"I don't either. Now look at this one of the car in the driveway. Do you see other violations here? In order to save time, let me point to the area I'd like you to focus on."

I point to the left rear of the car. I had noticed this last night, courtesy of a blown-up photograph that Sam had provided me. In normal size, I had looked at the photo three times before and not picked up on it.

"It looks like there might be a cracked taillight," she says, unable to conceal her surprise.

"Might be? Yes, that is a broken taillight. So just to sum up, the car next to the hydrant did not have a broken taillight, but the car in the driveway did?"

"If that's what it is, then yes."

"And the driveway photo was taken just hours after the hydrant photo? Early in the morning the next day?"

"Yes."

"So these are two different cars?"

"I can't say that."

"Let me rephrase. These are two different cars, unless on the way home that night Mr. Tierney either backed into a building or participated in a demolition derby?"

Vincent objects, but Judge Brickman overrules the objection.

"Officer Brock, let me put it simply. If the taillight was not broken between that night and the next morning, then it has to be two different cars. Is that correct?"

"I don't know that. The photo I took was taken at night, and it is a little blurry . . . dark . . . hard to see."

"Really? When I asked you earlier to tell me if you saw any other violations in the photograph, I don't recall you using the words *blurry, dark,* or *hard to see.* I can ask the court reporter to read your testimony back."

"I should have said that," she says, floundering.

"But you didn't." The truth is that the photo is somewhat dark and blurry, which unfortunately the jury can see for themselves.

"I didn't realize you were trying to trick me," Brock says.

"You think that 'Do you see any other violations?' is a trick question?"

Vincent objects that I'm badgering the witness. Duh. Where has Vincent been? Badgering is what I do; it's my default mode.

But Judge Brickman sustains the objection, and before I can ask another question, Brock says, "I saw a car parked by a hydrant and wrote out a ticket. I did my job."

"You were directed by a phone call from an anonymous person, no doubt outraged at a car being parked near a hydrant. You then went there and wrote the ticket. Is that an accurate recounting of what took place?"

"Yes."

"Thank you."

Vincent gets up quickly to try to repair the damage.

"Officer Brooks, when the owner of the car returned to it that night, he would have seen the ticket you wrote?"

"It was right on the windshield."

"Knowing that, is it possible that he panicked and did something to his own car to make it look different from the one you ticketed?"

"It's possible."

"Something like cracking a taillight?"

"Possibly."

"Is it hard to break a taillight if that's what you want to do?"

"Certainly not."

"Thank you. No further questions."

The testimony about the taillight was helpful to our side, but nowhere near determinative. It's unfortunate that Ryan didn't even know it was broken; if he did, he might have mentioned it to someone or made a service appointment to have it fixed. As it is, we have no independent corroboration that it was broken prior to the night of the murders.

Judge Brickman adjourns court early today. I can tell that it pains him to do it, but a juror has a prescheduled doctor's appointment that can't be changed.

I am happy with the delay; we need all the time we can get. Whatever is wrong with the juror, I hope it's not serious and I'm okay if it's contagious; that jury room can get stuffy.

'm feeling a little bit better about our case, but I'm a long way from confident.

The broken taillight added a generous helping of reasonable doubt, though Vincent had some success on redirect.

Hovering over everything is whether I can get testimony about Jason Shore into the case. That possibility took a huge leap forward with Randy Clemons's revelation about what his wife, Denise, said to him.

What I am not close to having is a motive for the murders of Stephen Pearson and Mike Shaffer. I assume it was a business disagreement; the two must have either crossed Jason Shore or somehow posed a danger to him. But I don't know what that could be.

So bottom line, Vincent has a motive to use against Ryan Tierney, and I have none to use against Jason Shore. That's a problem; for jurors to decide *who,* they like to know *why.*

At eight thirty, Sam calls from his vantage point outside the warehouse. "Andy, they're loading a truck; should be done in about a half hour. I can't be sure they'll stop at the diner, but it's worth a shot."

"I'm on the way." I grab the extra keys that had been in Ryan's house. "Call Laurie and tell her, and also give her the license number on the truck if you can see it." The keys have tags with the license numbers on them; if we know in advance we can save time.

"Will do."

On the way out I say, "Tara, don't wait up for me. And make sure Sonny brushes his teeth."

I head to the diner, trying not to go too far over the speed limit because the last thing I want is to be stopped by a cop tonight on my way to committing a felony. I get there in just under thirty minutes. Laurie somehow is already here, as is Sam. We park in the predesignated place.

"What's the status?" I ask.

"If he's going to be here, it will be in the next ten minutes."

"Let me have the keys," Laurie says, and when I give them to her, she finds the one that matches the license plate number Sam gave her. We're all ready to break into the truck; now all we need is the truck.

Sam was wrong; it takes fifteen long minutes, but the truck pulls in and parks in the back. We are not far off, shielded by cars, and we watch him carefully lock the thing up. He even walks around to the back and tries to open it by hand, to make sure it's really locked.

Laurie positions herself so that she can see if the driver is coming back, but is also close enough to us to intervene if we have a problem. For example, a major problem would be if there's another Pearson employee in the back of the truck.

Sam opens the back lock with the key and raises the door. He only opens it high enough for us to get inside; we're going to be shining lights in here, and the less it's seen by others the better.

The first thing I notice is that it's freezing in here; this is a refrigerated truck. It actually feels good compared to the summer heat outside.

Sam has sort of a flashlight/lantern that lights up the interior of the truck, and it has probably thirty boxes in it. They are all stamped with the words MEDICAL—HANDLE WITH CARE.

The boxes are all sealed tight, as I assumed they would be. "We're going to have to open a couple," I say.

"They'll be no way to conceal it. We don't have the right kind of tape; even if we reseal them, they'll know we were here."

"No, they'll know someone was here. They won't know it's us."

We pick two boxes, one from each side of the truck so hopefully they have different items inside. Sam hands me a box cutter and I open one of the boxes, while he opens the other one.

At first I recoil at what I see, but then I realize what I am looking at. They are prosthetic limbs of all different sizes; there must be fifty arms and legs in this box alone. I touch one, just to make sure that my original fear that they were real severed limbs is not warranted.

I go to another box and slice it open; it does not have any identifying writing on it. When I open it, I see some metal devices; I have no idea what they are, but I grab one.

"Wow," Sam says, from the other side of the truck. "This is amazing."

"Prosthetics?"

"Let's get out of here," he says, which is good enough for me. I grab an arm and a leg and we both jump out of the truck, closing the door behind us. There's no reason to take the time to lock it; they're going to know it was broken into based on the open boxes.

I signal to Laurie, and when she comes over, I say, "Let's meet at the house."

Nobody says another word; we go to our respective cars and we're out of here. I realize when I'm in my car that I still don't know what Sam saw, but I'm going to find out.

L aurie and I arrive at the house before Sam.

The dogs haven't had their nighttime walk and I'm sure they're anxious, but for now I just let them roam in the backyard for a few minutes to take the edge off.

Tara looks at me with disdain as if to say, *This is a one-shot deal, buddy. You are not getting out of walking us; I didn't sign on to hanging out in the backyard.* Little does she know that I like the walks almost as much as she does.

I put the prosthetic limbs and the metal device on the table for Laurie to see. "These were just two of the boxes; other ones could have been more of the same, or something else. I don't know what Sam saw, but he sounded stunned by it."

She touches the prosthetic limbs and picks up the metal device to examine it. At that moment I hear Sam's car pull up, and a few seconds later he's inside.

He looks at what is on the table. "Damn."

I point to the metal device and ask if either of them knows what it is.

"It's a bump stock," Laurie says.

"What is that?"

"You attach it to a semiautomatic firearm to make it fully automatic. It does it by harnessing the recoil energy and . . ." She stops when she sees by my face that I have no idea what she's talking about. "Never mind how it works; it creates automatic weapons."

"Why would someone need that?" I ask.

"Not for deer hunting."

"Sam, what did you see?"

"Pieces of armaments. Rifles, shoulder-fired missiles, and I'm sure much more."

"What does that mean, *pieces*?"

"They weren't assembled; they were literally in pieces."

"But you can tell what it was?"

Sam nods. "I'm sort of into that stuff."

"Sam, do you know where this truck is headed?" I ask.

"According to the logs, the pier in Baltimore."

"Why would they need to ship things internationally through Baltimore?" Laurie asks. "There's plenty of ports here they could go through."

"Maybe they have a way of evading inspection there. What I want to know is, where are they getting this stuff?"

"I think I may know," Laurie says. "Where's your computer?"

I take her into my office and log her into my computer. She starts typing keys and doing searches. Sam and I don't want to look over her shoulder, so we maintain a respectful distance and wait.

"They're printing it," Laurie finally says.

"Printing what?" I ask.

"Everything you saw in that truck."

"How?"

"It's called three-D printing; I just read an article on it. People think it's new, but it was actually invented in 1984. But when it comes to printing out something like a rifle, it does it in pieces. It can't print out the assembled unit. All of this is meant to be assembled at the destination."

"Damn, that's right," Sam says. "It's got to be; I've read about it also. But would it be illegal?"

"The arms definitely," I say. "And this other stuff, like the prosthetics, there would be patents on all of it. They're essentially setting up a black market in everything. And internationally as well. They can make a fortune."

Laurie adds, "That would explain what Sam said about the deliveries to the warehouse being huge, flat cartons. They're probably stainless steel or plastic strips. Then machines turn it into dust and it's fed into the printer and melted. You should read about it; the process is amazing."

"I can't print out an email," I say. "But this all makes sense. Now we have to figure out how to use it to help our client."

I think we finally uncovered the answer as to why Jason Shore invested that money in Pearson Trucking, without any obvious return.

So why am I not particularly happy about it?

It is not simply that happiness is not part of my personality, though for the most part it is not. It's more that while it seems like progress has been made, at this point it's an illusion.

To start with, we have no presentable evidence of what we learned last night. Even though there are prosthetic limbs and a bump stock sitting in my house at this very moment, I cannot show them to the authorities.

We didn't find them on the street; we illegally broke into a truck and stole them. Even if I were willing to admit that I committed that crime, the items themselves would be rejected as evidence for having been illegally obtained.

So our first task is to find a way to expose what Shore and Pearson are doing without revealing our activities last night. Unlike us, the police need real-life probable cause to enter that factory, or one of the trucks. They need a judge to sign a warrant, and at this point I don't see how we can provide the corroborating evidence to get that done.

Should we somehow accomplish that, our next job would be to get Judge Brickman to allow us to present it to the jury.

Here I am more optimistic; I think we have a compelling argument in that regard.

But assuming we clear hurdle number two, the toughest one remains. We would need to demonstrate that the illegal activity at Pearson is tied into the car explosion that killed three people. Just because Stephen Pearson was a crook, it doesn't necessarily follow that one of his fellow crooks killed him.

But for now I have to get through the conclusion of the prosecution's case. Vincent calls Dennis Giuli and immediately establishes him as the founder and owner of Giuli Fireworks, based in Elizabeth.

"Can we assume by the name of your company that you manufacture fireworks?"

Giuli nods. "Manufacture and distribute."

"Do you consider yourself an expert on explosives?"

"I'd better be; I deal with them enough."

"Is that a yes?"

"Yes."

"Do you know the defendant, Ryan Tierney?"

"Yes."

"How long have you known him?"

"Going on twenty years; we grew up together."

"Do you consider him an expert in explosives, if you know?"

"Definitely. Better than me."

"Again, if you know, how did he come about this knowledge?"

"It's something we always had an interest in; we actually took courses when we were younger. But then he was an ordnance expert in the army, so that took it to another level."

"In recent years, have you done business with Mr. Tierney?"

"Yes."

"Describe that business, please."

"I sell stuff . . . you know, fireworks . . . to Ryan whole-sale. And then he resells them. And he also does his own fire-works shows for companies, outings. . . . He even did them for Pearson.

"When he does those shows, he likes to make some of his own stuff, so I sell him the materials. I've been to a few of his shows; they're great."

Vincent gets Giuli to list a few of the specific explosives he provides and asks if they are powerful.

"You'd better believe it," Giuli says.

Vincent turns him over to me, and I start by asking, "Did you ever have reservations about making these sales to Mr. Tierney?"

"What do you mean?"

"Were you worried about what he might do with them?"

"No, not Ryan."

"You never feared he would do anything but make fire-works?"

"Right."

"If you wanted to blow up a car, triggered by turning on the ignition, are these the materials you would use?"

"No. There are much easier methods, ones much less likely to fail."

"Would Mr. Tierney be familiar with those other options?" He nods. "Sure he would."

"Would he have access to them?"

"You mean could he get them? Definitely. And if not, he could make them. I mean, they're just made up of chemicals. Ryan could do it in his sleep."

"Thank you."

I let Giuli off the stand and Vincent calls Captain Terry Stearns of the New Jersey State Police.

Captain Stearns is in charge of the bomb squad in the North Jersey area, and he says he's been on the job for twenty-eight years.

"That's a long time," Vincent says.

Stearns smiles. "Especially when you do what I do."

Vincent spends some time on the explosives that were used in the bombing, making sure the jury understands from Stearns that they were the same ones that the previous witness said he had sold to Ryan.

"Did you have occasion to visit the defendant's home?"

"I did. I was asked to go there the day after the bombing."

"Did you find explosive materials present there?"

"Yes. In the basement."

"What did you assume from what you saw?"

"It was a workshop. My assumption was that someone worked with these materials down there. Based on the setup and the safety precautions, it was clearly someone with significant knowledge of what he or she was dealing with."

"Were these materials the same ones used in the car bombing?"

Stearns nods. "Some of them were, yes."

On cross, I basically ask Stearns the same questions I asked Giuli. He is less inclined to follow my lead, which is not surprising. For example, when I ask if other materials would have been easier to use in the bombing, he says yes but qualifies by saying, "For someone who knows what they're doing, it really wouldn't matter much."

It's been a really bad day, one I have seen coming for a while. Ryan is an expert with explosive materials and had a basement full of the stuff that blew up the car. The car driven by the guy who had just fired him.

Karen Vincent is smart enough to know to quit when she's on top.

"Your Honor, the defense rests."

Judge Brickman turns to me. "Mr. Carpenter, be ready to call your first witness on Monday morning."

It's while I'm walking the dogs that I come up with a possible solution to the probable cause / search warrant problem.

I somehow need for the search to be executed in a place where searches do not require a warrant, where they are normal and legal. An airport is an example, but that doesn't work in this case because the Pearson trucks can't fly.

But that's not the only example. "Tara . . . Sonny . . . I think I know how to do this," I say. Neither of them respond, and Sonny pisses on a tree; it might be his subtle way of showing a lack of confidence in me.

But I am undeterred. "It can definitely work; the only problem is I have to call my father."

So as soon as we get home, I do just that, and after the *How are you?*'s, I say, "I need a favor."

"That's what I'm here for," he says.

"Can I come over?"

"Always."

"Can I bring the dogs? I sort of promised them I'd be with them all weekend."

"Of course. They're family."

We head over to my father's. Every time I enter Paterson I have the same reaction: I feel like I'm home. The overwhelming percentage of people, if given the choice between Franklin Lakes and Paterson, would choose Franklin Lakes.

Not me.

I revere my father, but he goes up yet another notch in my estimation when it turns out he has biscuits waiting for the dogs. They also seem quite pleased and surprised, and after he gives them a couple each, they lie down to sleep it off.

We go into the den to talk.

"So what's the favor?"

"Actually, there are two of them. The first is for you to do something based on something I know, and the second is for you not to ask me how I know it."

"That makes it a little tougher. I'll do my best."

"Thanks. A while back, when I was working in the office, I believe you had a case that caused you to work with US Customs and Border Authority."

"Yes. On more than one occasion."

"Do you still have contacts there?"

"I haven't spoken to anyone there in a long time, but I could certainly resurrect what was an excellent working relationship. I'm sure some of the people are still there."

"Good. There is going to be a truck, probably tomorrow night or soon after, that is going to leave the Pearson warehouse in Parsippany and head to the pier in Baltimore. It will be carrying goods that will need to be processed through Customs before leaving the country."

"Okay," he says, waiting.

"Included in those goods will be material that should not be leaving the country, goods that were illegally manufactured in violation of numerous patents.

"I believe that the reason the goods are being shipped through Baltimore, rather than the many closer ports, is that some arrangements are made with pier personnel to sneak them through and evade inspection. I want officers waiting to uncover the conspiracy and confiscate the goods."

"But you can't tell me how you know this."

"Correct, but that is only the first step. Very quickly after this is accomplished, they need to get a search warrant to enter the company's warehouse in Parsippany. That is where all this stuff is made."

"What do you mean by 'made'?"

"Three-D printing."

"I have no idea what that is."

"Join the club."

"When will you know when the truck is en route?"

"When it leaves the warehouse, maybe even before that."

"They are going to ask me how I know this."

"You can tell them the truth; that you heard it from a confidential informant. Just don't mention that you used to change the informant's diapers."

He smiles. "Maybe twice."

"They don't need probable cause. They just need to trust you. They're allowed to search any cargo that comes through the port."

"They will trust me."

"There's one more thing," I say.

"Uh-oh."

"I need whoever is in charge to agree to testify in my trial. Just to whatever events happen at the port and the warehouse."

"If it all works the way you say, that shouldn't be a problem. They will be very grateful for the tip and subsequent arrests. If it doesn't work the way you say, you won't want them to testify anyway."

"Okay, so you'll do all of this?"

"You know I will."

've decided not to call to the court's attention in advance that I am going to be bringing Jason Shore into the trial.

I'm just going to do it, and if there's a fight to be had, I'll have it when it comes up. But I think I'm on solid legal ground, which will get even more solid as evidence is introduced.

My first witness is Anna Pearson. I don't know if she conspired in the murder of her husband, but I think she certainly went along with it. But I'm not going to accuse her now because I don't have the evidence. That may come later; for now I am just going to use her to bring in Jason Shore.

If she lies and denies everything, then I have the tape of her conversation to use against her. She doesn't know I have it, and I am secretly hoping I get to use it. Demonstrating perjury by the owner of Pearson Trucking would be a good way to kick this off.

I've gotten a voice expert to analyze the tape and certify that it's actually Anna Pearson and that the conversation is legitimate. I have an affidavit from the expert, and he is available to testify if I need him. Billy Cameron is not going to like the amount of money the expert charged for his work.

She takes the witness stand, and I approach. For now I have to be fairly gentle with her; she's the wife of the victim and as such has jury sympathy built in.

"Mrs. Pearson, you are now the sole owner of Pearson Trucking since your husband, Stephen, passed way?"

"Yes, but he didn't just pass away. He was murdered."

I nod. "Which is why we are here. Were you very involved with the company before Stephen's death?"

"No. He would occasionally talk to me about things, maybe bounce some ideas off me, but not frequently."

"Have you familiarized yourself with the operation since then?"

"Yes, somewhat."

"Do you remember the two times we met prior to today?"

"Yes."

"Both times were at your house?"

"Yes."

"The first time I asked you if the name Jason Shore was familiar to you? Do you remember that?"

"Yes."

"The second time, weeks later, I came back and asked you the same question, and I mentioned that I had information that he had invested more than two million dollars in Pearson Trucking, and— . . ."

Karen Vincent interrupts me and asks that we have a meeting in chambers. Judge Brickman grants the request and we head back there. Whenever I go to a judge's chambers, I feel like I'm going to the principal's office.

Once we're back there, Judge Brickman says, "Ms. Vincent, you have the floor."

"Thank you, Your Honor. I felt it was important to interrupt the proceedings to object to what I can see coming. Mr. Carpenter is going to bring in irrelevant information, as part of a fishing expedition, to unfairly malign Jason Shore, and either directly or indirectly imply that he might be involved in this crime. I should point out that there is absolutely no evidence of that, but plenty that points to Ryan Tierney."

"Mr. Carpenter?" the judge asks.

"Your Honor, what Ms. Vincent has just said is so ridiculous I am amazed and impressed that she said it with a straight face. She actually is asking you to prevent us from preventing evidence while claiming we have no evidence.

"Pearson Trucking is a criminal enterprise. Four people have been murdered, the three in the explosion whose deaths we are dealing with here, and the person that took over for Pearson, Mike Shaffer.

"But there is a wider conspiracy going on, which I will have conclusive evidence of very soon . . . within days. It is impossible to see all this going on and not consider its potential relevance. This is information the jury needs to have."

We kick it around awhile longer, but as I expected, the judge lets me bring it all in, though he tells me he will be watching and will have me on a short leash if I go too far afield.

We go back to the courtroom and I repeat and finish my last question to Anna Pearson. "When we met the second time, I again asked you if you were familiar with Jason Shore. I said that I had information that he had invested more than two million dollars in Pearson Trucking and asked if you knew that. Do you remember this?"

"Yes."

"What did you say?"

"That I had since learned about Mr. Shore's involvement and that investment. I also said there was nothing illegal about it."

Damn. I'm not going to get to use the tape. She's too afraid she'd get caught perjuring herself. I wonder if she cleared this burst of honesty with Jason Shore.

"To your knowledge, has any portion of the investment been repaid in the last two years?"

"It has not."

"Does Mr. Shore now own a part of the company?"

"No. But he believes in its long-term future."

"Isn't that nice." Out of the corner of my eye I can see Vincent about to object, but she changes her mind. I don't think "annoying sarcasm" is a legal objection.

I take out documents from the Pearson financial records showing the investments by Shore. I show them to Anna and they are also shown on a video screen that is set up.

Sam had obtained this stuff illegally, but I've since subpoenaed them so that I can use them in court.

Anna identifies the line items that show the four investments, which amount to more than $2 million. "And you have testified that Mr. Shore made those investments?"

"Yes."

"How were these investments physically made? Did he write a check?" I ask this even though it clearly shows on the documents that it was a wire transfer.

"No, they were wire transfers."

"This number here next to each wire transfer . . . twelve digits long . . . what is that?"

"I don't know."

"It's always the same number, correct?"

"Apparently."

"I don't see Mr. Shore's name on these documents. He made an effort to conceal his involvement?"

"You would have to ask Mr. Shore that."

"I look forward to that. No further questions."

Next I call Lieutenant Pete Stanton to the stand.

The idea of testifying as part of the defense case is horrifying to Pete, and he had told me that if I called him, he would dismember my body and spread the pieces all over New Jersey.

That seemed to be a bit of a harsh overreaction, so I convinced him to testify by telling him exactly what I wanted from him on the stand, which in no way forces him to voice an opinion favorable to the defense.

I also agreed to buy him food and beer at Charlie's in perpetuity, but I'm confident I can successfully renege on that in the future.

Once I ask him to identify himself and present his exemplary record, I ask him about the night in the Franklin Lakes park: "You were in that park that night?"

"Yes, along with the Franklin Lakes Police."

"Why were you there?"

"A friend in Franklin Lakes PD called me as a courtesy and gave me a heads-up. He was aware that I knew you and that you were from Paterson." Pete goes on to say that the two deceased men were armed, and that one had been killed by a single bullet in the side of the head, and the other by blunt force trauma to the head.

"Has the person who killed them been identified?"

"No."

"What are the names of the deceased?"

"Samuel Cawdrey and James Parker."

I show Pete and the jury documents included in the discovery information I received from that night. They show that Cawdrey and Parker both received $25,000 in a wire transfer two days before they died.

I also get him to point out that the account numbers on the wire transfer are the same as the ones on Shore's investment in Pearson Trucking.

"I asked you to look into what this means. Did you do that?"

"Yes. It means that the same entity sent all of those wire transfers."

"Can it be learned who controls that entity?"

"No. The transfers are from the Cayman Islands and are untraceable and secret."

"So if Jason Shore or an entity he controlled, as described by Anna Pearson, sent the investment money, then he or an entity he controls sent the money to these two men as well?"

"It would appear that way."

"I am involved with a Pearson Trucking case, and two armed men waiting for me in the park were paid by an investor in Pearson Trucking. Does that strike you as too much to be a coincidence?"

"It would be, but you said that night that the men have nothing to do with you."

"Obviously I was wrong. Thank you, Lieutenant; no further questions."

Karen Vincent gets up, frowning that she has to deal with this nonsense. She is dismissive of Pete on cross. "Lieutenant Stanton, do you have any knowledge of a connection between what happened in the Franklin Lakes park and the murders of Stephen Pearson, Denise Clemons, and Donald Muncy?"

"I do not."

"Thank you."

As I'm leaving court, I get a call from Sam. I've been waiting for this call for three days.

"According to the logs, there's a truck leaving the warehouse now that is scheduled to go to the port in Baltimore. It takes a little over three hours to get there, but he may stop along the way."

"Do you have the license number?"

He gives it to me and I tell him to call me if he gets any information updating the situation.

As soon as I hang up, I call my father and tell him exactly what Sam told me, including the plate number on the truck. He tells me that he will call his contacts, who have been waiting for three days as well.

"Okay, thanks. It's important that they prevent the driver from notifying his people as to what is going on. When they execute the warrant on the warehouse, I don't want them to have been tipped off so that they can clean up the place."

"Yes, sir. Any other instructions?" I can almost see my father smiling as he says it.

"No, you can take it from here."

"Thank you. By the way, could you be wrong about this truck?"

"Yes. It's certainly possible."

"Okay, here goes. It turns out the most embarrassing moment of my career may take place after I retired."

know what the old saying is, but it turns out that a watched phone does ring.

The call I've been desperate to receive from my father finally comes at ten thirty:

"It went down exactly as you predicted. Cargo is what you thought plus more . . . dental implants, machinery, drugs . . ."

"Drugs?"

"Yes, apparently you can make the casings with three-D printing. Anyway, they impounded it all and arrested the driver."

"Terrific. Are they getting a warrant?"

"Got it already and will be executing it soon, alongside the New Jersey State Police."

"Terrific. And you didn't get embarrassed," I say.

"Embarrassed? This is the proudest of you that I've been since you hit that grand slam home run against Clifton to win the game."

"There was no home run. I struck out with the bases loaded, Dad."

"You can't allow your aging father his fantasy?"

The second call comes at 4:00 A.M. I can't believe my father is still awake, though he does seem to be loving this time back in the action.

"Search was a total success; they were shocked at the size of the operation. It's padlocked and being analyzed, and arrest warrants are out for Jason Shore and a guy named Kenneth Burks."

"That's his right-hand man."

"He's going to be his cellmate after this."

I hang up and resist the urge to call Laurie, though I want to share this with her. I don't want to wake her, and I think on some level I am afraid a guy will answer the phone.

I don't know why that would bother me; it shouldn't.

But it would.

I can't go back to sleep, and the dogs are zonked out and clearly not in the mood for a walk, so I turn on the television to see if they're reporting anything on the raid.

They're not, so I just watch the local news, which consists of identical weather reports every four minutes. In between are traffic reports and items that I have no interest in. For some reason these stations no longer have sports reporters; maybe they've ceded that territory to ESPN.

Finally I call Laurie at seven thirty, and she's happy to hear about the night's events. "Can you use it at trial?" she asks.

"Once I get the details, you'd better believe it."

"You know, for the first time I'm pretty sure our boy is innocent. But that ups the stakes, doesn't it?"

I know what she means. If Ryan didn't do it, then it becomes absolutely imperative that he does not spend his life in jail.

"Welcome to the dark side," I say. "Can you deal with my father while I'm in court?"

"Deal with him how?"

"Find out as much information about the raid as you can, but most importantly, as part of the deal to give the cops the tip about Shore, they agreed to testify in the trial. I want to make that happen no later than tomorrow morning."

"Okay, I'm on it."

When I get to court, I spend a few minutes with Ryan, updating him on what is going on. I hadn't talked to him about the 3D printing, and he says he has absolutely no knowledge of it.

"But that would explain a lot, wouldn't it?"

"Hopefully."

"But why did they kill Stephen and Shaffer?"

That is the key question; he's asked it and I can't answer it.

From the mouths of clients . . .

My first witness today is Randy Clemons.

Somehow in the courtroom he looks even larger than he did the previous times I met him. Maybe that's because most of the time we were in his gym, which has a lot of large people running around.

He's wearing a suit that is so tight it looks like he was poured into it. He is only limping slightly, which I notice because I know that under one of those pant legs is a prosthetic device. It's metal, unlike the ones on the truck. I doubt the jurors can notice the limp at all.

I take Clemons through his work history as a cop; he was a detective working vice. He's an impressive guy and I certainly believe the jury will accept him as credible.

"Are you still on the force?"

"No, I lost my left leg in the line of duty. It was a raid gone wrong, although we did make the arrests."

"Do you miss being on the force?"

"Every day. But I can't do a desk job; it's not for me."

"Your wife, Denise, is one of the victims in this case, correct? She was in the car with Stephen Pearson and Donald Muncy?"

"Yes."

"Did you know those two men?"

"To a degree. I'd met them a number of times at company functions; they both seemed like nice guys."

"What did Denise do at the company?"

"She started out in accounting, but I guess Stephen realized how valuable she was and he started using her as his assistant. So she was involved in a lot of different things, backing him up."

"You came to see me last week, correct?"

"Yes."

"What was the purpose of your visit?"

"To tell you that Denise had told me that Stephen Pearson was very worried about a man named Jason Shore. He was an investor in the company."

"Can you be more specific? How and why was he worried?"

"I don't why; if Denise knew, she didn't say. But she told me that Stephen believed Shore was a violent man with frightening connections, and that he was very dangerous. For some reason he was upset with Stephen."

"Before that meeting last week we had met two times before, correct?"

"Yes."

"Why didn't you tell me this during our first two meetings? Or why didn't you go to the police with this information a long time ago?"

Clemons frowns. "I should have. But I assumed the defendant was guilty, and I didn't want to do anything that might get him off. It was stupid of me."

"Why did you change your mind and come forward?"

"Mike Shaffer's death."

Vincent immediately objects and we go to the bench for a conference.

"Your Honor, the Shaffer murder has nothing to do with this case," Vincent says. "It was a robbery, pure and simple. It is far more prejudicial than probative."

I smile. "Last I heard they hadn't solved the crime. Does Ms. Vincent have information that says it was a simple robbery? If so, she should share it and also let us know how she knows it's unrelated to this case."

"The burden is not on me," she says. "It's on the defense to show relevance."

I shake my head. "Your Honor, it should come in for a number of reasons, but the current one is that it was a motive for this witness to come forward. Without that, his reasons for his delayed recounting could be questioned by the jury."

"I'll allow it," Judge Brickman says. "But don't dwell on it."

"You mentioned the death of Mike Shaffer," I say to Clemons when we start again. "Who is he?"

"He was the number-two guy at Pearson and he was recently killed at his office. The newspapers said it was in the evening, and he was shot."

"Why did that cause you to come forward?"

"It just seemed like too much of a coincidence, and that maybe I was wrong in keeping quiet. This way all the facts would be out there."

"Thank you," I say, and turn him over to Vincent.

"Mr. Clemons, when Denise told you about Mr. Pearson being concerned about Jason Shore, did you advise her to go to the police?"

"No."

"Did she advise Mr. Pearson to go to the police?"

"I don't believe so."

"You're a cop. In the case of a deadly threat, should the authorities be involved?"

"Yes. I probably should have pursued it. If Denise had been worried for herself, I would have."

"Do you have any specific knowledge connecting Jason

Shore to this case, beyond this secondhand account describing Stephen Pearson as worried?"

"No."

"Thank you."

My next witness is Detective Scott Leeman, who works under Pete Stanton in Homicide at the Paterson PD. Leeman is in charge of the investigation of the Mike Shaffer homicide.

His is a straightforward presentation, describing how Shaffer was murdered at his office, and that the safe was open, apparently robbed by the murderer.

"Do you know how much money was taken?" I ask.

He shakes his head. "No, but they are said to have kept a very considerable amount of cash there. It was used for bonuses for the drivers and other employees, as well as purchases of merchandise. There could have been other uses, but I am not prepared to make that accusation without evidence."

"So no idea how much?"

"Based on what we've been told by employees, it could have been in excess of two hundred thousand dollars."

I don't mention that I know that Stephen Pearson had a need for substantial cash to fund his gambling activities. The office safe would have been a logical place to keep it, and Willie Tirico had said that in fact was the case.

"Was Mr. Shaffer's car parked at the office when he was found?"

"No."

"So is it your theory that he was driven there by the murderer, forced to open the safe, and then killed?"

"That's a possibility, but we have no confirmation of it."

"Is it also a possibility that the entire thing was made to look like a robbery, but that the murder was the goal all along?"

"I really couldn't say at this point; the investigation is on-going."

I let Leeman off the stand, and at the lunch break I head out into the hall to call Laurie, only to find her in the back of the courtroom. I'm not sure when she arrived; I hadn't noticed her before.

"Where are we?" I ask.

"The New Jersey State Police captain will be here tomorrow morning, but he's tied up until then."

"So I can't go over his testimony in advance?"

"No."

I'm not happy about this, but there's nothing I can do about it, and just having him here will be a major plus.

When court resumes I call for a conference with Judge Brickman and Karen Vincent during which I request a continuance until tomorrow.

Judge Brickman is always disinclined to grant any delays, but I tell him there have been major new developments in the case, and that a New Jersey State Police captain who can explain it all will not be available until then.

"It's my last witness, Your Honor."

The judge has no choice but to grant the request, and he does, so we're out of here for the day.

Laurie is still here, so I say, "Let's meet at the house."

Laurie updates me on what she learned from my father and from the Jersey State cop.

From my standpoint it could not have gone better, and I'm already looking forward to tomorrow in court.

I will have no trouble convincing the jury and any fair-minded listeners that Pearson and Shore were involved in a criminal conspiracy. The tough part will be getting them to believe that someone other than Ryan Tierney blew up that car.

Laurie leaves and I go into the den to relax and watch some television. Tara assumes the lap-lying, head-petting position, which remains incredibly comforting.

CNN is reporting that Jason Shore and an associate, Kenneth Burks, have been arrested in what they are describing as a Customs violation. I know it is obviously much more than that, but maybe that's all the authorities want to release right now.

I'm worried that the witness tomorrow won't go further than that, which would be a major blow to our side. I'm going to press him hard if he resists.

There is another negative to the Shore arrest. There is now no chance to get him on the stand; he would refuse to put himself in jeopardy, and the judge would support it. Even if he came in, he would just take the Fifth, as is his right.

On the positive side, the thought of Shore in handcuffs is extremely pleasant and satisfying. I'm not even feeling guilty about rejoicing in his pain; the guy did try to have me killed.

I've decided not to have Ryan testify in his own defense. We've talked about it a few times, and though he has the final say in the matter, he's said he'll go along with whatever I think is best.

There are just too many dangers in having him take the stand, with little upside. He doesn't have any exculpatory information to offer, and his denying guilt would be expected and therefore meaningless.

One way or the other, the defense rests tomorrow.

Captain Dennis Costello of the New Jersey State Police shows up just a few minutes before the start of court.

We barely have time to say hello before he's taking his seat on the witness stand and I'm ready with my first question. This is a potential lawyer's nightmare; we lawyers like to know exactly what our own witnesses are going to say.

But my concerns turn out to be unwarranted. Costello's testimony goes more smoothly than that of most rehearsed witnesses. He's obviously testified many times before and knows how to connect with a jury.

His description of Shore's operation is, if anything, over-the-top. Of course, the bigger it is the more credit he gets for bringing it down, and he makes it sound like a criminal conspiracy for the ages.

After having him fully describe the events both at the pier and then at the warehouse, plus the subsequent arrests of Shore and Kenneth Burks, I ask him how much money they could have made if their crimes had gone on.

"Many millions," he says. "They were setting up black markets all over the world, using products they had no rights to. And they were basically in the early stages; we uncovered plans to set up other printing warehouses, and not just in this country.

"This operation, as huge as it was, was really just a test to give them a blueprint for widening their reach and scope."

Karen Vincent takes the same approach to Costello as she has to the other defense witnesses, claiming that while it's all interesting, it has nothing to do with the case against Ryan Tierney.

"Captain Costello, do you feel like you wandered into the wrong trial?"

"Not sure I understand the question."

"Well, this is a murder trial, with three victims, blown up in a car bombing. Yet you said absolutely nothing about that in your testimony."

"I answered the questions I was asked."

"I'm sorry, I should have said that Mr. Carpenter asked you absolutely nothing about those murders."

"That's out of my control."

"Agreed. So let me ask you: Can you shed any light on what the jury will have to decide? Do you have any information at all concerning our case?"

"I do not."

"Well, what you did have to say was fascinating. Congratulations on the arrests, and thank you for the diversion."

She lets Costello off the stand, and Judge Brickman turns to me.

I take a deep breath and say, "Your Honor, the defense rests."

It's the first time I've ever said those words, and it was like chewing poison. It signifies that I have no bullets left in the defense gun, that this is as good as it gets.

It feels like a loss of control, though the truth is that criminals' lawyers never really have control. We are spin doctors, and at some point the spinning has to stop.

Ugh.

"Ladies and gentlemen, I have this thing that I do at the end of every trial," Vincent says, starting her closing argument.

"I do it to guide me in future trials, and it helps me live up to my responsibility to you and to the system we live by.

"I get the court transcript of my opening statement to see if we delivered on what I said would take place. I never want to overpromise, I want to be as honest as I can and tell you the facts as I see them.

"In this case, I think we were accurate. I told you that we would prove beyond a reasonable doubt that Ryan Tierney committed this crime, and I believe we did.

"I said that he left a calling card, and he did, though in this case it was a 'calling car.' Mr. Carpenter hides behind a blurry, dark photo of a taillight, but you know whose car that was. And you know that the defendant could have broken the taillight deliberately after seeing the ticket to cover himself.

"The license plate is also in that photo, and the ticketing officer wrote it down contemporaneously. That was Mr. Tierney's car near Morelli's Restaurant; no doubt about it.

"I also told you that we would show motive, even though we didn't have to. Ryan Tierney was fired by Stephen Pearson, and he swore revenge, and he got that revenge.

"I told you that we would show that Mr. Tierney is an expert in the type of explosives that were used, and you've seen that to be the case. We also showed conclusively that he was in possession of those explosives.

"I also told you about circumstantial evidence, and how significant it could be, even more so than eyewitness testimony. And you've seen that; in this case that circumstantial evidence is so compelling that I would submit there is only one conclusion for you to draw.

"What I didn't tell you, because I couldn't have known, was the tale that Mr. Carpenter would spin. No explanations, no refutations, just a fascinating story about Jason Shore and a trucking company that he tried to portray as a modern-day version of the Corleone family.

"But in that entire story, did he once tell you why anyone would have wanted Stephen Pearson dead? According to Mr. Carpenter, Pearson was a coconspirator with Mr. Shore. Mr. Shore needed him and his company, so much so that he put up two million dollars to be a part of it.

"Why kill him? And why kill Mr. Shaffer, who by the way was murdered in an obvious robbery. An empty and open safe is usually a dead giveaway that a robbery has taken place.

"Maybe Mr. Shore is a criminal, but he will have his day in court, just like Mr. Tierney is having now. But if Mr. Shore's defense rests on an irrelevant narrative like Mr. Tierney's does, I would say he's in trouble.

"I told you in my opening that your job was a tough one, but very important. Now it's time for you to do that job. Follow the evidence. Follow the facts. Thank you."

I stand to give my closing argument. I haven't rehearsed it; I never did when I was on the other side, and I'm not starting now. I know what I want to say, so all I have to do is get up and say it.

"Well, this is it . . . we're all in the homestretch. All you have to do is listen to me babble some more, then pay attention to Judge Brickman's instructions, and then it's in your hands.

"Ms. Vincent just said you have a tough and important job. That's something that we lawyers always say to juries; sometimes we believe it and sometimes we're trying to butter you up. But we always say it.

"So I'm going to break a cardinal lawyering rule and tell you that your job is not so tough, not this time. Important? Yes. Tough? No.

"You know what would be tough? If you had to go back in that jury room and decide who killed Stephen Pearson and Denise Clemons and Donald Muncy. That would be damn tough, and I'm glad I don't have to do it because I have lived this case since the beginning, and I couldn't answer that question. I think I know—at least I think I know who ordered it—but I am not sure beyond a reasonable doubt.

"But I do know one thing; when it comes to the question of Ryan Tierney, you are bathing in reasonable doubt. Pearson Trucking, from the moment Jason Shore poured money into it, was and is a criminal enterprise. Shore put in millions, not out of the goodness of his heart, but because he expected to make many more millions.

"Of course, not all criminals who do illegal acts to make money are killers. But let me tell you something: there are killers out there. Someone killed Mike Shaffer and someone sent two armed people into the park near my house to wait for me. And someone killed those two people.

"I'll tell who didn't do all that: the one person who couldn't have is Ryan Tierney. Because he's been in jail, accused of a crime he did not commit.

"Ryan Tierney represented the perfect fall guy. What Ms. Vincent would have you believe is conclusive circumstantial evidence is a created illusion. He was an explosives expert, which was known because he did fireworks shows for the company? Then let's use a bomb.

"He had an argument with Stephen Pearson? Perfect . . . he's our man. Even the car, which the taillight proved was not his, could easily have been faked. This was not a Maserati, there are thousands of cars like that on the street. One could have been stolen, or rented, or painted.

"And the license plate? You don't think they could have made a duplicate? These are people who could print anything.

"There is simply no way you can know with certainty that Ryan Tierney, with no criminal past and no violence in his background, who served his country admirably, committed this crime.

"So please go back there, do your important job, and let Ryan Tierney move on with his life.

"Thank you."

And that's it. It's out of my hands. I'm a spectator. It is the worst feeling in the world.

've been following your case," Nicole says when she calls. "It seems like you are doing wonderfully."

"Only if we win. There's no middle ground."

"The pressure must be intense."

"It is now. This is the worst part because there is nothing to do but wait."

"Andy, what has happened to us. What are we doing?"

When she says this, I finally realize how angry I am. Maybe the pressure of the trial is making it worse; I'm not sure. "We're not doing anything, Nicole. I'm here and you're there."

"I don't want it to be this way."

"That's your call. And I'm not going to accept that my career is the problem. I wasn't an English professor or a CEO or a hockey player when we got married, I was a criminal attorney. I was trying to put people in jail rather than keeping them out, but that is a distinction without a difference. That's what I was and that's what I am."

"I know that."

"Then you either accept it, or you don't."

"You're very angry with me."

"For now, but I'll get over it, because I still love you. But you need to decide if you want me, or some other version of me. And if you decide you want out, I won't be angry. It's your right, and maybe you made a mistake, and this is you correcting it."

"Andy—"

I interrupt, "But this revolving-door stuff is bullshit, and I'm done with it."

"Fair enough. I need to think and take a hard look at myself, and at us. And if I come back, it won't be halfway."

"Good."

When I get off the phone, I ask Tara, "What do you think? Will she come back?"

Tara is noncommittal about it, but I'm sure she wants Nicole back. It doubles the number of human hands that can pet Tara and certainly increases the amount of biscuits she receives. Tara is nothing if not logical, and self-centered.

I've always hated waiting for verdicts, but this is going to take it to a whole new level. In the past, I was rooting for a guilty verdict, and the pressure was worrying that I didn't do enough, and a criminal would be let back on the street.

But in this case, if we lose, Ryan's life is effectively over. And I think that would be unjust; I do not believe he did the crime. I would have to live with it every day for the rest of my life, while his disappears day by day.

Laurie calls and asks if I'm okay. "This waiting is going to be awful," she says.

"Tell me about it."

"I've enjoyed working with you. I appreciate it."

"I hope that doesn't mean you're resigning. I'm going to have more cases, and I could never find a better investigator than you."

"I'll be here."

"Good. You know, in addition to the torture of waiting

for the verdict, there's another thing that bothers me, that I didn't expect."

"What's that?"

"There's a mental void in terms of the work. I've been trying to solve a puzzle all this time, and that's over. There's no reason to solve it anymore because there's no jury to show what I come up with."

"I know what you mean," she says.

"When I was in the prosecutor's office, I moved on to the next case. There was no shortage of criminals to be put away. I would think the same thing would be true of you as a cop."

"Very much so." Then, "Will you call me when you hear something? And certainly when there's a verdict?"

"I will."

We hang up, and I do what I should not do, which is try to put myself in the minds of the jurors. It does me no good; I have no idea what they are thinking.

I think we have a good reasonable-doubt case. I don't think all twelve jurors will buy our argument, but I think a hung jury is possible. I also don't think all twelve will go along with the prosecution's case, but you never know. Sometimes a herd mentality takes over, and the jurors fall into line behind a guilty verdict.

I know it doesn't matter anymore, but I wish I knew why Stephen Pearson had to be killed. What happened to cause Shore to have the bomb placed in that car?

I'm frustrated, and anxious, and a nervous wreck.

This is a fun job.

I do not want there to be a quick verdict, but I also want the agony of waiting to be over.

I know . . . it's a contradiction.

But I just cannot see the jurors quickly coming back with a verdict of acquittal, so I think the longer it goes the better. On the other hand, and there always is another hand, there could come a point when the holdouts might get sick of holding out and join the mob.

The jury has now been out for two days. I've spent that time visiting my client, who makes me look calm and serene by comparison, and walking the dogs. I've walked them so many times for so long that their paw pads must be worn down.

It used to be that I would grab the leash and Tara and Sonny would jump up, excited at the prospect of going out. Now they just lie there and Tara looks at me as if to say, *You need to get a life, buddy.*

There really should be a course taught in law school called Verdict Waiting 101, because nothing has prepared me for this.

Laurie, using her contacts, has been following the cases against Jason Shore and Kenneth Burks. They're out on very high bail, but because they are both considered flight risks, they are in home confinement with ankle bracelets, and their passports have been taken away.

I'm sure the police must be monitoring and restricting their communications with everyone but their lawyers, so, for example, if they tried to hire a hit man to kill me, we'd know about it.

I've been to Charlie's a couple of times in the hope that I could divert myself with sports. Both times Pete Stanton was there, and I've gotten stuck talking to him and paying his tab. I never saw anyone eat that much; I think he starves himself until I show up. But if I keep going there, I'm going to have to take out a mortgage.

I was there last night and he wanted to talk about the case, which made one of us. "You think you're going to win?" he asked.

"Absolutely maybe."

He shook his head. "You're going down in flames."

"It's always a treat to talk to you."

"You want to know why I say that?"

"Not even a little bit."

He ignored that. "Because you didn't give the jury a reason for Shore to kill Pearson."

I didn't argue the point because Pete was right. So instead I said, "Check, please," to the waiter and got the hell out of there.

Among the things I still don't know is Anna Pearson's role in this. Was she an active participant, or did she just acquiesce in the murder of her husband? He did cheat on her repeatedly; maybe she just decided she was fine getting rid of him and starting over.

And Mike Shaffer is a bigger mystery. Why kill him? He

was obviously doing Shore's bidding once Stephen Pearson was killed. Maybe Shore believed my bullshit story about Shaffer revealing Shore's investment to me. But that seems a flimsy reason to kill him.

Also, staging the Shaffer killing to look like a robbery was a pretty feeble and uncharacteristic effort by Shore to evade suspicion.

The person I feel most sorry for in this whole thing, besides Ryan, is Sharon Muncy. She lost her husband, has a small child to care for, and didn't get the life insurance money the company promised her. I will have to look into that.

But that is going to have to wait. My phone rings while I am walking the dogs. I hope it's a telemarketer, but the caller ID says PASSAIC COUNTY. For a brief instant I don't want to answer it, but I know I have to.

"Hello?"

"Andy, it's Rita Gordon." Rita is the court clerk.

"I hope you're just calling to chat."

"I am. And my conversational opener is 'Get your ass down here, there's a verdict.'"

In all the trials I handled as a prosecutor, I never once showed up at court for the verdict thinking I was going to lose.

That just wasn't part of the mindset. We had the evidence, we presented it competently, and it was going to carry the day. It didn't always work out that way, but it usually did, and we always, always thought we would win.

Today is the first time I'm waiting for the verdict as a defense attorney.

I think we're going to lose.

The verdict has come too fast; it seemed like it took forever, but it was little more than two days. We needed it to go longer, or for them to come back after a week and say they could not come to a decision.

I'm at the defense table when Ryan is brought in. It's just the two of us, and I look over and the prosecution side is packed with lawyers. I had hoped the jury would look at the difference and see us as the little guy, trying to take on the big, bad system. Right now I don't think that's what they thought at all.

It seems to take forever for Judge Brickman to enter the courtroom. For the entire trial he treated every minute as if it was precious, and now I can picture him in his chambers getting a mani-pedi. He needs to get the hell out here.

Ryan is clearly having difficulty with the stress. He's not

saying anything, not even asking me what I think is going to happen. He's managing to stay composed, but it must be a struggle.

Karen Vincent comes over to shake my hand. She says, "No matter how this turns out, we fought the good fight."

I just nod; I have nothing to say, mostly because my throat feels like it's gripped in a vise.

Finally the judge comes in and asks that the jury be brought in. As they are entering, some are looking at Ryan and some are not. I have no idea what that means.

Ryan leans over to me and says, "You did great . . . thank you." Then he takes a deep breath and awaits his fate.

Judge Brickman asks the jury if they've reached a verdict, and in my mind I'm screaming, *Of course they have, asshole! That's why we're here!*

But fortunately my mouth remains closed, and after the foreman says that they have indeed reached a verdict, he hands it to the bailiff, who brings it to the judge to read.

Judge Brickman's face betrays nothing as he hands it back to the bailiff, who brings it to the court clerk to read. The judge asks Ryan to stand, and both he and I do. I can't even feel my legs; I don't know how Ryan can get out of his chair.

This process could have taken seconds; instead it feels like it's taken a couple of months.

Finally, the clerk starts to read . . . "We the jury, in the case of the *State of New Jersey versus Ryan Tierney*, find the defendant, Ryan Tierney, as it relates to the charge of murder in the first degree of Stephen Pearson, not guilty."

I'm stunned, and I listen carefully as the other counts are read. There is no way Ryan can be not guilty of killing Stephen Pearson, but guilty of killing Denise Clemons or Donald Muncy, but still I want to listen to make sure.

When the final not guilty verdicts are read, Ryan hugs me and says, "I can't believe it," and I say, "Join the club." He then sits down. I think it's to prevent himself from fainting.

The judge thanks the jury and tells Ryan that he is free to go. The gallery is loud; I think they're as amazed as I am. I turn and see Laurie back there, smiling and giving me a thumbs-up.

And then she mouths, *We did it.*

I swear, I think Sonny knows what's happening.

He looks more chipper this morning, and when we go on our walk, there is more of a bounce in his step. He's enjoyed his stay here, but on some level he knows he's going home today.

Tara, for her part, seems fine with it. She's been okay with Sonny, but they're not as bonded as it seemed like they were on the day I got them out of the shelter. I think Tara prefers humans.

Laurie wanted to be here for the reunion. She's a tough, no-nonsense ex-cop, but in real life she's a softie. So we wait for Ryan to arrive to reconnect with his buddy.

It's worth the wait; Sonny goes nuts when he sees him, running to him, tail wagging a mile a minute. Ryan gets on the floor with him, petting and laughing. It's great to see.

We settle in the kitchen with coffee to talk, while the dogs eat their biscuits. I can't help wondering what Nicole would think if she walked in at this moment on me with Laurie and a guy accused of mass murder . . . all in her kitchen.

"I can't believe you won," Ryan says. "I am so grateful to both of you."

"We all won," I say. "You did your part by being innocent."

He smiles. "It was the least I could do. And I can't thank you enough for saving Sonny. If he had to spend all this time in that place . . ."

"He didn't," I say. "And he was a perfect tenant here."

The conversation drifts to the case, and Ryan once again asks why I think Pearson and Shaffer were killed.

"I don't know; that's been confusing all along. I can only assume Pearson turned on Shore in some fashion. I think Anna must have been on board, so that Shore knew he could rely on her after Pearson and Shaffer were gone."

"I meant to ask, was Anna at the party that night? She obviously wasn't in the car," Ryan says.

"I'm sure she wasn't there," I say. "Was it normal for spouses to attend?"

He nods. "Most of the time. Stephen encouraged it; he saw them as extended company family."

"Maybe Stephen was meeting another woman afterward at that apartment," Laurie said.

"Or maybe not," I say, suddenly realizing what has been in front of me the whole time. "Ryan, are you aware of a promise the company made to provide a life insurance policy for its employees?"

"Sure; Shaffer sent around an email a long time ago. We had to tell them a beneficiary."

"Sharon Muncy told me Shaffer reneged on the promise."

Ryan frowns. "That sounds like him."

"Laurie, I need you to go back to talk to the night doorman at Hudson Towers."

"What for?"

"To show him a photograph."

I'm back at Gilmore's Gym for the third time.

Except for the gym at Eastside High School, it has now moved into first place in terms of total gym visits for me. But it's fair to say that as often as I have now been here, I have neither worked up a sweat nor had a wheat germ smoothie.

It's 11:00 A.M., which I have come to understand is Randy Clemons's preferred workout time. Sure enough, he is doing bench presses when I arrive. I don't know how much weight is on those barbells, but I couldn't pick them up with a forklift.

Unlike the previous times, he smiles when he sees me. "Congratulations, Counselor, you did good."

I return the smile. "And you helped a lot. But now I need something else from you. Smoothie, anyone?"

He nods and we head into the small café area. He goes to the counter and gets his smoothie and brings it back to the table. "So how can I help?"

"First, a quick question. Did you drop Denise off at Morelli's that night?"

"No, she drove."

"What happened to her car?"

"I picked it up at the restaurant a couple of days later. Why?"

"That's what I figured. So what I need is for you to give me the cash you stole from the Pearson safe when you killed Mike Shaffer."

"What the hell does that mean?"

"Which part didn't you understand?"

"I didn't kill Mike Shaffer, and you—"

I interrupt, "Not only did you kill Mike Shaffer, but you also killed Stephen Pearson, Don Muncy, and your wife."

"You're insane."

"And you're stupid. You left so many clues I'm surprised I didn't trip over them. The wife you said you loved was sleeping with Stephen Pearson. She wasn't coming home that night, and you know how I know? Because you told me that they woke you in the morning to tell you she was dead.

"But you hadn't been calling the police when she didn't come home that night because you knew she wasn't planning to. The doorman at their little love nest recognized her photo.

"The restaurant owner said that Denise did not look drunk that night, because she wasn't. She wasn't with Pearson because she was in no condition to drive. She was with him because she was going with him to his apartment."

Clemons doesn't say anything, so I go on.

"Maybe she was planning to leave you, but either way you couldn't stand it. It made you less of a man. So you killed them both. Then when Mike Shaffer told you he was reneging on the life insurance promise, you killed him and took the money out of the safe."

He's looking furious, like he's going to explode and kill me. I'm just glad Laurie is outside, armed and waiting for a signal.

"Which brings me to why I'm here. I want that money. I get it, and you never hear another word from me. I did my job and got my client off; I don't give a shit one way or the other about you."

"I'm listening."

"I thought you would be. I'm planning to be in the food court at the Paramus Park shopping center at five P.M. It will be crowded, so you won't try anything. Bring a suitcase with the cash in it, and our relationship ends there. Otherwise, I go to the cops, and believe me, I can prove everything.

"I'll be in my office until then. Call me to confirm that you're coming. I don't want to waste my time; the food there is not that good. But it's a hell of a lot better than wheat germ, which, by the way, I don't believe they serve in state prison."

I slide a piece of paper across the table with my office phone number on it.

"If you don't call by five, don't call at all. It will be too late."

I get up and leave. The conversation did not go as well as I had hoped; I'm wearing a wire and I wanted him to say something incriminating. But he didn't; what little he said constituted a denial.

But I feel more certain than before the meeting that I am right. Clemons planted that bomb and also killed Mike Shaffer.

Now all I can do is go back to the office and wait to see if he calls.

The time is moving slowly; it's only been two and half hours, but it seems like a month.

I have no idea if Clemons will call. I certainly think he would trade the money for getting off the hook for the murders, but he might not trust me to keep my end of the bargain.

He might also think that I'm bluffing about having the proof, and he'd be mostly right about that. If that's his view, he could think he could survive an investigation once I made the charge. I doubt that he could; once the police had him in their crosshairs, things could come out. But I'm not sure.

Just in case, Laurie's friend Marcus is assessing the situation at the food court. It would seem that Clemons would not try any violence there; it would be crowded at that hour. But Marcus would be there to intervene, and as he showed in the Franklin Lakes park, he's an extraordinary intervenor.

I'm sure Clemons has been spending these hours assessing his options. He had to be stunned to realize that I was onto him, and until recently he was right to be unconcerned.

I'm not sure why he chose to come forward to testify for the defense during the trial. After setting up Ryan so perfectly, it represented an about-face.

Maybe Shaffer's revelation that he had reneged on the life insurance put Clemons over the edge. Or maybe he knew that he couldn't pin Shaffer's murder on Ryan, so he wanted to make Jason Shore the certain fall guy.

But now the ball is totally in his court; it's his decision to make.

He's going to lose whatever he decides.

And then I hear the noise from downstairs. Someone has opened the door and entered the stairwell.

I don't know for sure if it's Clemons, but that's the way to bet. And there is nothing for me to do but wait.

Having anticipated this possibility, I'm in Sam's office, and he's here with me. That puts me even closer to the stairs than if I were in my office, so I can clearly hear as the person I think is Clemons makes his way up the steps.

One of the advantages of having an office in an aging dump is that the stairs creak, so when it stops, I know that he's made it to the second floor. I'm sure he's walking down toward my office, and I'm also sure he must be holding a handgun.

But I'm afraid to look.

A minute goes by that feels like a hundred minutes. I'm afraid he might hear my heart pounding and follow the noise back to Sam's office.

"Freeze, Clemons!"

It's a man's voice, but it's clear that Clemons must not have obeyed, because two shots ring out. Then I hear some screaming, so much so that I can't make out individual words. One of the voices is Laurie's.

I assume it's over, but you couldn't pry me out of Sam's office with a can opener. "Let's get out there," Sam says, but my legs are nailed to the floor.

Finally the door opens and it's Laurie. "We're done here," she says.

We go out and see that the hallway and my office are crawling with cops. Medics are attending to a person on the ground; I hope and assume it's Clemons.

"Is he going to be okay?" I ask.

Laurie shrugs. "Who cares?"

My investigator is not a shrinking violet.

Pete Stanton is here as well. "Nice work."

"Thanks. But if you'd arrested the right person in the first place, we wouldn't have to go through this."

"You won one case," he says. "You'll lose the next ten."

"Do you need me here right now?"

"No, but come down to the precinct later and make a statement."

I promise to do that, but first I have something to attend to.

Anna Pearson doesn't seem surprised to see me when she answers the door.

"I was hoping not to see you again."

"You're not the first woman to say that to me. Can I come in?"

She sighs and steps aside, which is as good an invitation as I am going to get. I follow her in and she leads me into the den. No offer of coffee this time; she's hoping for a quick meeting.

"I should thank you for identifying Stephen's killer," she says.

"Yes, you should."

She doesn't say anything for a while and I don't either. Finally she says, "Are you going to tell me what you want?"

"Oh, I was waiting for you to thank me. I want a check for seven hundred and fifty thousand dollars."

"What?" she asks, apparently shocked.

"Which part didn't you hear?"

"Are you trying to extort me?"

I shrug. "Sort of. Your company promised life insurance policies to your employees, but didn't deliver, so Sharon Muncy hasn't gotten what she is due. I figure a million dollars ought to cover it."

"Now it's a million? I thought it was seven fifty."

"It just went up; I'm a sucker for round numbers."

"Why would I go along with this?"

"The company, which you own in its entirety, promised the life insurance policies in writing. A good lawyer, which I coincidentally happen to be, can take you to court and force you to pay.

"In the process, I will work to make sure that certain things come out."

"Like what?"

"You are connected to Jason Shore. I've already proven that, as you know. And he was very confident he could continue doing his business with your company after your husband and Shaffer were killed. You probably brought Shore into the company in the first place. I'll expose everything publicly while I take you to the legal cleaners."

She doesn't say anything, probably considering her options, of which she has none.

I break the silence. "Make the check out to Sharon Muncy."

head down to the precinct to dictate and sign my statement about what happened today.

Laurie is here when I arrive, and she fills me in on the current status. Clemons has been taken to the hospital with a bullet wound in the chest. It's serious, but the early assessment is that he will survive.

Once I'm done with the statement, I say to Laurie, "Will you take a ride with me?"

"Where to?"

"I'll tell you on the way."

Sharon Muncy greets us at the door, carrying her daughter, the same as last time. That little girl's feet must never hit the floor. "Oh," she says, clearly not expecting us.

She invites us in and, when we sit down, says, "So Ryan was found not guilty."

"Yes," I say.

"Will we ever know who killed Don?"

"We know that already," Laurie says. "It was Randy Clemons, Denise's husband."

"What?" Sharon asks, obviously shocked. "Why did he do it?"

I explain it as best I can, and then she asks, "So did you come here to tell me that?"

"No, we came to give you this." I hand her a sealed envelope with the check inside, and she asks if she should open it. "Please do."

She opens it, looks inside. "Oh, my God . . ."

We tell her that the money came from Pearson, and it represents the life insurance money that she was entitled to. "We would have sued them for the money, but Anna Pearson realized they would lose in court."

"You don't know what this means to us," Sharon finally says. She then starts to cry, which makes me tell her we have to go. I hate crying, no matter who is doing it, whether it's from good or bad news.

When we get back in the car, Laurie asks me about how Clemons managed to frame Ryan. "Whose car was it by the hydrant?"

"I don't know. My guess is it was stolen or rented. If it was stolen, Clemons might even have painted it. And he probably snuck into Ryan's driveway and took off the plates, then put them back later. He could have done that without being detected. Or maybe he somehow made new plates. He is resourceful."

A few minutes later, as we're driving, I see Laurie break into a wide smile.

"What is it?"

"Since I started working with you, I've looked the other way when you and Sam committed cybercrime. I've been a lookout when you broke into a truck. It's been quite a ride."

"Having fun?"

"Prior to this the worst thing I had ever done was copy an answer on a third-grade spelling test from Freddie Gerber. And I confessed to the teacher without being caught."

"Why did you look the other way when Sam and I did this stuff?"

"I guess I wanted to see justice done."

"Welcome to the dark side."

I know some things, but not everything.

I know that I have found my calling. The case and trial were simultaneously torturous and invigorating. I was engaged in a way I never had been before. I cannot imagine ever wanting to retire.

I know I have found a perfect investigator and partner in Laurie Collins. She is great on many, many levels. We are almost totally in sync, and when we're not, we adjust.

I know I need some office help. I am going to call that woman Edna . . . she's been described as a dynamo, and that's what I need. I also know I need to get a coffee machine.

I know getting Tara was maybe the best decision I have ever made or maybe ever will make.

I don't know what is going to happen with Nicole. I love her and I hope she comes back, but I do not like where we are or what we have become.

But you can't know everything.

ABOUT THE AUTHOR

Brandy Allen

David Rosenfelt is the Edgar Award–nominated and Shamus Award–winning author of more than thirty Andy Carpenter novels, including *Dog Day Afternoon*; several stand-alone thrillers; nonfiction titles; and several K Team novels, a series featuring some of the characters from the Andy Carpenter series. After years of living in California, he and his wife moved to Maine with twenty-five of the four thousand dogs they have rescued.